The Secret

of

the Garden

By

Ronna M. Bacon

I do not pray for these alone, but also for those who will believe in Me through their word. John 17:20.

Table of Contents

Chapter 1

She stood in the overgrown, worn-out garden, her eyes searching through the debris. It was here somewhere, she knew, that secret her mother had told her about as a child. She just had to find it, but where? That was the million dollar question, she thought. She wiped her brow, then stared at the muddy mark on her wrist, the sweat on her brow turning the dirt to mud. Great, she thought, just what I needed. I only have a limited amount of time today and this was not part of it. I had not planned on digging through dirt or debris.

She spun slowly in a circle, before trudging back to the edge of the garden along the narrow path she had managed to chop out, turning to get her bearings. What was it Mom had said, she questioned herself. Something about the centre of the garden and a stone or statue or something. There's nothing here now. And who knows where it would be. This garden is so overgrown, it looks as if I'm going to have to clean it up before I can even make a proper search.

Sighing with fatigue, Faith Webster moved towards the faded, tired, worn-out house that belonged to her now. Not that she wanted it. Not a chance, she thought. I want to live in the city, not in some hick town, away out in the boonies. She paused as she stared at the steps, worn and tired, just as she felt, as a fleeting memory tugged at the edge of her mind, something that made her feel happy for a few seconds before it disappeared.

Mom, you need to be here, but I know you can't. That hip surgery of yours is taking too long to heal. I need you with me, but I don't know why. I'm scared, and I know I shouldn't be. Why, Lord? She silently screamed at Him as she raised her face to the setting sun. Why am I here? You know I don't like this place and haven't since the accident all those years ago. Is that why You brought me here, to deal with that? I could have done without that, you know.

She trudged up the steps, fatigue pulling her down. She stopped once more to turn and stare back over the property. I really don't need this land, Lord, so why am I here? She headed across the wooden porch, intent on cleaning up and finding something to eat. Only, I'm too tired to eat. It's early but it's been a long emotional day, a long emotional week. No, make that a long emotional month with too much going on for me to handle, she thought. Tears sparkled on her cheeks before she raised her open hands to swipe at them.

A noise behind stilled her forward walk, and she paused, listening intently, before she shrugged and reached for the door knob. A sudden rush of noise and she was slammed bodily against the door, her head twisted sideways as an arm thrust against her neck.

She screamed before she was pulled away from the door, an arm wrapped around her, trapping her arms against her body and a hand slapped viciously across her mouth. She fought her attacker, fear rising within her.

A guttural voice sounded loud in her ears, asking her where it was. She shook her head, not knowing what he meant.

"What was in the garden? Where is it? It's mine and I want it."

She shook in her terror and then anger. She fought against her captor, her heels kicking at his legs, struggling to escape. His hand loosened enough she was able to clamp her teeth into the fatty fingers.

With a shout of rage, the man shook her, her teeth rattling against one another before he slammed her into the clapboard walls. Her head thudded dully against the wood and she slumped to the porch floor, her movements stirring up dust and old dried leaves. Spiders scurried away to hide, and a mouse peeked through a hole in the floor before it too disappeared to safety.

He stood, her assailant, eyes filled with rage and hatred, and then his foot came back as he kicked at her. He shoved open the back door that led to the large, old-fashioned kitchen, his eyes searching through the destruction he had caused there while she had been in the garden, not finding what he wanted. He paused as he heard a truck engine and stomped to the front window.

Just great, he thought. Now I have another one to get rid of. He watched as a young man slid from behind the wheel, pulling off his baseball cap before he settled it once more on his head and stood, staring around the overgrown yard as the rays of the setting sun cast a reddish glow over him. The mind started for the stairs at the front, moving in a tired manner and as if he had no real desire to be at that very place.

The man in the house watched, finally yanking open the front door and charging towards the man, surprise on his side. He launched himself forward, catching the younger man in the chest and sending him backwards from the next to last stair, to land harshly on the flagstone path. The older man rose, fists ready but not needed, as the younger man sprawled, unconscious, in front of him. He stared around, finally heading down the short lane and to his car he had hidden in a grove of trees not far from the lane entrance. Anger and hatred warred with one another inside him. Which would win?

Chapter 2

A hand held to the back of his pounding head, Seth Logan sat upright, his stomach roiling with the pain. Now, what did I go and do, he thought? I just don't remember that fight, if that's what is was. Looking through blurry vision, he sighed as he remembered. Yeah, he thought, the old Webster place. I was here for a reason, but I just can't think of it right now. Put it this way, head, you're making it difficult to think at all. He rose cautiously, pain wracking through his body. How far did I actually fall, he thought, before he headed for the porch and the front door.

He knocked, then banged on the door, with no response. He stepped to the edge of the porch, one arm circling a post, while the other hand on the railing balanced him, and he looked around. He was right. There was a car there. Someone should be here but they're not answering. Early dusk had fallen, making it difficult for him to see.

He sighed, the sound loud in the night. He tilted his head for a moment, enjoying the sounds of the night, the twittering of birds settling down, the bullfrogs in the creek behind the house, the night birds calling to one another, the rustling of little critters, the humming of insects. He turned, heading for the back door. He had always liked this place, the wraparound port a favourite of his.

He paused as he saw a dark form on the floor, near the back door. He frowned, not quite sure what he was getting into. He walked cautiously forward and nudged the body with the toe of his booted foot, and then dropped to his knees. Memory assailed him as he sat for a moment, memory of finding his sister just like this, and the agony of not knowing if she would even live or die from the sudden heart attack she had just a few years ago. Too young for it, they said, but it happens. He snorted. Sure it happens, Lord. But not to me. Not to my sister.

His hand touched the back of the person, relief coursing through him as he felt the rise and fall of the body. Gently, he reached to turn the body over, shock running through him at finding a female. He sat back for a moment, his thoughts confused, then realized she must be the one he had come to see. What was her name again? Oh, yeah, Faith Webster, namesake to the previous owner, who had passed away recently and left this property to her only granddaughter.

He rose, reaching through the open door to flick on the porch light, frowning as the moths flocked to the light. He dropped down once more, his hands assessing her, before he scooped her into his arms and headed into the house, stopping in surprise at the ransacked rooms. She wouldn't have done that, he thought. Must have been whoever it was that knocked me cold.

He laid her gently on the couch in the kitchen, and then shoving aside debris with his foot, knelt again to assess her. A dark bruise discoloured her forehead. She seemed to be breathing okay, he thought, and rose, heading for the sink, praying that there was water running. He opened the tap, running the water until it was as cold as he could get it, searching a nearby drawer until he found a cloth, wringing it out under the tap, before the tap was off and he was back beside the young woman, the cloth folded on her forehead. She hadn't awakened and that worried him.

He rose, reaching for his phone, and calling for help. His father would come, he knew. A retired paramedic, he still monitored the calls, ready to lend aid if needed.

Seth stood for a moment, his eyes on her before he strode away, searching through the two stories of the house for anyone hiding. This is strange, he thought. The upstairs wasn't touched. I can see which room she chose to use, her luggage is there.

He walked quietly back down the old oak stairs, creaks sounding under his feet. He loved the sound of the movement of old homes.

He heard a sound from the kitchen and headed that way, finding the cloth flung across the room and the young woman sitting up, her head in her hands.

She looked up at him through dark brown eyes, pain etched in them and on her face, her golden blond hairs mussed.

"Just why did you hit me?"

Seth stared at her for a moment. Shaking his head and regretting that very movement, he spoke. "That wasn't me. He nailed me as I was coming up the front stairs. I have no idea who it was."

She frowned. "Are you sure? Someone knocked me out." She stared around the room. "What happened? I was in the garden for a couple of hours and I know I didn't leave the room like this."

Seth gave a grim smile. "The downstairs had been tossed, as they say. Upstairs is fine." He held up a hand at her glare. "I had to search the place, you know, to make sure someone wasn't hiding here."

She stood, her legs trembling under her, shaking off the hand he reached out to help her. She managed to walk to the counter, where she held on, afraid her legs would give way and she tumble to the floor.

"Thank you, then." The words were grudgingly given, and she turned, frowning at him as she heard him give a sound.

The sound of sirens split through the darkening night air, and she sighed. "You just had to call them, didn't you? I could have done without."

Seth stared at her, his mouth open before he clapped it shut. "Listen. I came here as a neighbour and because my Dad asked that I do, as a courtesy to your grandmother, who was a good friend of his." He strode through the house, opening the door for the paramedics, greeting them as old friends, and then reaching to shake the hand of the responding officer.

"Todd, thanks for coming. It's strange, what's happened."

Todd nodded, his eyes assessing the rooms. "She didn't do this, did she?"

Seth stared at him, even as he heard the conversation in the kitchen, Faith denying she needed to be assessed, the paramedics finally convincing her she needed to be. "What did you say?"

"She's not happy, you know. Mom spoke to her mother. They're old friends. Her mother said she didn't want the property, didn't want to live in the boonies as she put it, and why did her grandmother have to do this, anyway?" Todd Wilson's voice was low but held a touch of amusement as he quoted Faith's words.

Seth shook his head again, his hand going up to press against his temple. Todd's hand came out to steady him before he directed him to the kitchen.

"Sit. You need to be checked out as well. While we're waiting, fill me in."

Seth submitted to the examination, shaking off the request that he go with them to the hospital, his eyes on Faith, watching as she sat, her eyes on the debris and shambles of her house. He sighed to himself, knowing he was committed to helping her.

A hand landed on his shoulder, and he looked up to see his father, Joseph, standing beside him.

"Can we talk, son?"

Seth rose, following his father to his truck, where Joseph leaned against the hood, his eyes on the distance.

"Talk to me, son. There's more you're not saying/"

Seth nodded, his arms stretched out on the metal of the truck. "I never saw him, Dad. He jumped me and knocked me flat. When I walked around the porch and found her, all I could see of was Anna and how I found her."

Joseph heard the sounds in his son's voice, the despair and anguish rising in it. His hand landed once more on Seth's shoulder.

"I understand that, son. But what happened with Faith? What did she say?"

Seth shook his head, dropping his forehead to his arms. "She thought I had hurt her, Dad. You know me. I couldn't hurt a lady."

"I know that, son. She will too. She'll be here for a while, I'm thinking."

"And why would that be?" A female voice sounded behind him, bewilderment, grief and almost anger in it."

Joseph turned, not able to assess Faith as he wanted to. "You can't leave now, not until the investigation is done, and that moves real slow hereabouts. Besides, you have to rehabilitate the house, I'm given to understand.

She stood, arms folded against her, the gentle night breeze blowing her hair across her face before she reached and captured it in one slim hand.

"Unfortunately, what you say is true. I'm sorry. Have we met?"

"Years ago. I'm Joseph Logan, your neighbour. Your grandmother was a good friend to my family."

"It seems she was a good friend to a lot of people, but not a good relative. Thank you for stopping by. Don't let me keep you." She spun on her heel and walked rapidly back to the house, the two men hearing the door slam and the sharp click of a lock.

Joseph and Seth stared at each other, not quite sure what she meant. Seth sighed, his eyes going to the lights in the house.

"I'm staying here tonight, Dad. I can't leave her, not with what happened."

Joseph nodded. "I thought that's what you'd say. I have a thermos of coffee and some sandwiches in a cooler with me. Your mom packed them. Let's pray for her first, though, son. Something's going on with her, and I have no reading on what it could be."

Seth nodded, his head bowing as he heard his father's prayer, finally looking back at the house as he took the small soft-sided cooler and the thermos of coffee.

"Call me if you need me, son. Watch your back." Joseph drove away, his brake lights blinking on and off, a bright red in the dark night.

Seth settled down in his truck, and then not satisfied with that, grabbed the blanket he kept in his truck and the thermos of coffee and headed for the front porch. He settled down in an old wicker chair, his phone on the small table beside him. He didn't think he sleep, but the headache and pain he felt finally drove him to close his eyes.

He didn't see the shadow that approached, stopping in its forward movement as he was spotted. The shadow waited before moving away. The man would be back on another day, and when he returned, she would tell him what he wanted to know and how to find the treasure he had been told was buried in the garden. He needed that statue or fountain or whatever it

was he had heard her muttering about being
missing. That was the key to his fortune, he
decided.

Chapter 3

Flicking open the curtains in the front room as she called it, the parlour she knew her grandmother had called it, Faith stood for a moment, enjoying the warmth of the early morning sun as it rose, bright red. Another hot day, she thought. I need my air conditioning. She knew she'd be spending a portion of the day in the garden, as well as trying to straighten up the house. It was Saturday, and she usually spent it running errands, having lunch with friends, preparing her lesson for her preteen Sunday school girls. That was not happening today, and she wanted that routine back. She needed that routine. It made her feel safe, and right now she didn't feel safe.

She grabbed the broom from where it was stored in the front closet and pulled open the door, already reaching to wipe off cobwebs, her motions freezing as she saw the man huddled under a blanket, still asleep. Afraid for a moment, she slowly approached, then stopped. Seth Logan. He had spent the night out here, making sure she was safe. She paused in her anger, knowing it wasn't justified, not towards him. Yes, Lord, I get it. I have to apologize to him, and I will. But why did he stay? After what I said last night? You know, Lord, this has stirred up too many memories and hurt.

Seth stirred, his eyes cracking open, catching sight of Faith standing there, broom half raised, a faraway look on her face as she stared past him.

"Morning." His voice held that early morning, gravely sound.

She jumped, the broom clattering to the floor, sending the sparrows in the nearby spirea bush fluttering away, their angry chatter loud in the air.

"I'm sorry. I didn't mean to startle you." Seth sat up, pulling the blanket from around him, and folding it neatly, setting it on the table beside him, reaching to pocket his phone. He would check it later. He knew either his mother or his father would have sent a text late last night and early this morning, just checking to see if everything was still quiet.

"You did, you know. You have a habit of that." She frowned at him. "Did you sleep out here in that old chair all night?"

He nodded as he squinted in the sun. "I did. Someone had to. It was more comfortable that my front truck seat."

"You shouldn't have." She spun, took a step, and then turned back. "I'm sorry. That wasn't nice of me. Thank you. I also apologize for last night. I wasn't nice then either."

Seth stood, his height surprising her once again. All the men in her life seemed short compared to him. "It's okay. I know you were scared and hurt." He looked around. "Look, it's Saturday. I'm not working, so let me stay for a little while at least and help you."

She pondered his offer, not quite sure if she should take him up on it, then shrugged. "Whatever. I have bread and eggs, if you want breakfast. And coffee, I think, was packed in a box by my Dad. Not sure if there's cream, but I think I remember putting some into the fridge."

Seth began to laugh, drawing her eyes to his slate coloured eyes and red gold hair. He picked up her broom, setting it tidily by the door and then motioned for her to enter the house.

"Show me where the food is and I'll cook, if you want to clean up. I don't think you did that last night, now did you?"

She looked down at her rumpled dirty clothes and sighed. "No. I think I planned to but dropped to the bed, wanting to rest for a moment. The next thing, I knew it was morning." She stared at the lawn, what she could see through the window, and reached to grasp his arms, her fingers tight on it. "Seth, did you walk around the house during the night?"

He shook his head, his eyes following her. "Those are footsteps. Stay here. I'll take a look."

He came back presently, a grim look on his face. "Someone was around again last night. They didn't come near the house, likely because they saw me." He pointe inside. "Can we find that coffee and talk, perhaps?"

"Sure. It's on the counter. I dug it out while I was waiting for you." She spun and ran up the stairs, her thoughts in a jumble. She wasn't used to this, not since she had moved out on her own. She could come and go, she thought, not having to depend on anyone or answer to anyone.

Seth watched her run away, knowing that was exactly what she was doing. He shook his head, a smile on his face, as he headed for the kitchen, starting the coffee, then staring around.

He reached for dishes and platters and silverware tossed on the floor, setting them in the sink. Food items were stacked into the cupboards and pantry. He finally reached outside for the garbage can, sweeping all the broken items and dust and debris up and dumping it into the can. At least one room was clean, he thought, as he poured his coffee, reaching for the bread and eggs, seeing sliced ham and veggies in the fridge as well. An omelet, he thought, or a western sandwich. Either would work.

He turned as he heard soft footsteps, then an exclamation behind him.

"What did you do, Seth? Clean the kitchen for me?" She was astounded, not having friends that would have done that for her.

He grinned. "I had to. It's the way I was raised. Besides we couldn't eat in the clutter." He drew back a chair for her and made a small bow. "Your seating awaits you, my lady."

She stared at him once more, then smiled. "Thank you, kind sir." She looked past him at the living room and sighed. "I have four more rooms down here to sort through and then I need to work on the garden."

"Eat." He pointed at her food. "Let's work outside first, before it gets too hot. I think that's what did you in yesterday, wasn't it?"

She finally nodded. "It was. Who was it, Seth? Who attacked both of us?"

He shrugged. "I have no idea, Faith. I wish I did." He ate for a while, his thoughts not on the food but on the lady across from him. None of the neighbours knew much about her, other than what her grandmother had said, and that was little. He vaguely remembered hearing about an accident or something years ago, but nothing had ever been said since then.

He frowned, bringing her eyes to him, a questioning look on her face.

"Seth? Why the frown? Do you have to leave? If you do, that's fine." She knew she was stammering and stuttering, and that she really didn't want him to go but would never say anything to him to keep him there.

He looked up, a smile brightening his face. "No, I'm good for the day. I was just thinking about something."

"Well, then, stop. I don't like your frown."

Seth started laughing as he gathered their plates and utensils and washed them, the frying pan he used hitting the water as well. He turned, seeing her beside him, drying the dishes and putting them away, a vision catching at him and stopping him in his tracks, of Faith and him doing this every day. Now, where did that come from, he asked himself? She's going to sell the house and move back to the city.

Faith turned, walking to the kitchen doorway, staring at the living room, and knowing Seth was right. This could wait, couldn't it, Lord? Why am I all of a sudden so confident in a man's direction, in a suggestion that is not an order?

She headed for the backyard, finally, finding Seth was already there, having found the tools they needed and loaded them into the wheelbarrow. He stood, arms crossed, head tilted, the sun reflecting gold on his hair. He pointed with his chin.

"So, where do you want to start?"

She snorted, not very ladylike, he thought. "I have no idea. I garden, but only in well behaved gardens. This was certainly is not."

"Not, it's not. I suggest I start with cutting away as much as I can, if you can manage the wheelbarrow. Your grandmother had a burn pile near the creek. We can dump the debris there for now." He reached for his gloves and then paused. "Before we start, Faith, I would like to pray, asking for protection. It's how I start any work I do."

She looked startled, then nodded. "Of course, Seth. Lead away on that."

Hours later, Faith stood, sweat on her face that she rubbed away on her T-shirt shoulder. "I think we've done as much as we can today, Seth. Thank you."

He looked up, a grin on his face. "I think we have. Let me put everything away." He paused, his eyes uncertain, something she had come to recognize in just those few hours was not him. "Mom sent a text and asked if you would like to come for supper. It's a simple supper, but it's your choice."

She shook her head. "Thank your mother for me, but I think I need to stay here." She looked back at the house. "I have some things I need to do. Thank you for your help today."

She watched as he nodded, and then finally drove away. She sighed. She didn't need any more complications in her life, and he would be a big one, she thought, if she let him.

She returned to the house, a sigh coming from her as she contemplated the living room, before reaching for books that had been pulled from the shelves. Darkness had fallen by the time she had straightened up the downstairs. She looked towards the kitchen, then shook her head. No supper, she decided. Not tonight. She locked up the house, heading for the upstairs, then returned to the doors, contemplating the old-fashioned deadbolts, before slamming them home. She touched the windows, finding them locked, and turned once more, still not comfortable in her safety. This is silly, she thought. I should be comfortable here, but I'm not.

Lord, protect me this night, please. I have no idea what is ahead of me, but I can feel fear and terror rising within me. I thought I had conquered that, but I guess I haven't.

She rose the next morning, and sat on her back porch, contemplating the garden, before she rose and walked to it, into the centre where a mark showed an object had sat there for years. What it was, now she could not remember. She would need to call her mother, she decided. She might remember but then again she might not. She could not remember seeing it there when she used to visit as a child but then she had found, sometimes childhood memories are not reliable. And that hurt in more ways than one.

She sighed before walking the worn path to the creek, hearing the morning birds and insects, seeing rustling in the grass from rabbits and mice, she supposed, feeling the sun on her face. She stood for a while before heading back to the house. It was Sunday and she should be in church, that was expected of her, but not today. Today, she would spend the day here, just waiting on God to speak to her, showing her the plan He had for her. But then again, that was not likely to happen. He had not done that so far, regarding this property. She had done what was expected of her and she could feel the rebellion rising in her.

Seth sat restlessly in the back pew, his mind not totally on the message his friend was preaching that day. His thoughts kept going to the young woman he had spent the day before. He had caught traces of humour from her, but more than that, he had found sadness and uncertainty and doubt. He wanted to know her better, to see what was behind her pretty face, and wanted to help her, and that he wasn't sure how it work out. She had mentioned that she needed to get the house ready to be sold, that she had commitments in her town she needed to get back.

He rose, his father finding him. "Seth?"

"Yeah, Dad?"

"You're unsettled this morning. Want to talk about it?" His eyes studied his son, concern and love warring in his glance.

Seth shook his head. "Not really. I'm not too sure what I want to do. But Faith needs our prayers. There's something more going on with her, other than the assault."

Joseph nodded. "Your mother is planning on dropping in on her tomorrow. Let her talk to her. She may be able to find out something. In the meantime, we can pray for her."

Seth eyed his father, knowing there was more behind his words than what he had said. "I know, Dad, and thanks. Listen, I'm heading off now. John asked if I could stop by for a while. He's been laid up now for so long, he wants some company." His friend, John, had been housebound due to a broken leg and was just now getting his feet back under him.

Joseph nodded as he watched his son walk away, sudden apprehension and fear for him filling his heart. He turned as he felt a hand tuck into his arm. Martha stood here, her eyes on her son as well

"What's going on, Joseph?"

Joseph shrugged as they walked towards the car. "Just not sure what's going on, love. I feel danger in the air around him, and I don't know why."

She nodded. "I think the same. All we can do is pray for both of them." She buckled her seatbelt, her eyes on the horizon. "We need to get to know this young lady, Joseph. Her life is about to become entwined with his. And that is concerning."

"It is and I have been." Joseph paused in his words, a sudden chill running through him, and reached for his wife's hand, hers gripping his tightly, both knowing their son was walking into something that they could not prevent or save him from.

Chapter 4

*F*ear took hold of Faith the next morning as she stood, coffee mug in hand, staring at her garden. Yes, she was not seeing things. There were fresh footsteps there, not hers and not Seth's. Someone had been around during the night. She spun, her eyes searching desperately around her, not seeing anyone, but feeling like she had eyes on her. And that she did not like one bit. She threw away her coffee, suddenly having no taste for it, and ran for the house, fear rising in her.

Lord, what now? Why am I here? And who is after me? I know someone is, and I don't know who or why.

She stood in the living room, her eyes closed, trying to calm herself and knowing that it wasn't working. Mom, I need you right now. I need to hear your voice and your prayers. But I can't call you. You're not here and I can't have you worried. Not when you need to heal. And Dad is so worried about you, I can't call him. Tears sprang to her eyes and overflowed, causing her to drop to her knees, her hands over her face.

How long she stayed there, she was never sure afterwards, but she felt a peace and comfort flow through her. She knew her mother was praying for her, she could always feel her mother's prayers. She finally rose, her eyes searching the rooms.

"I need to get busy." She spoke to herself, longing for someone to talk to.

A sound at the door had her frowning. She approached it, standing to one side to look out the etched window in the door. Seeing nothing, she reached to unlock it, and then, still seeing nothing, her hand on it to close it, she felt something brush against her ankle. She jumped, her hand going to her chest as she looked down, a softening on her face. A little black and white puppy stood there, her eyes on Faith before she jumped to lick her hand.

Faith dropped her knees, giggles breaking from her as the puppy licked at he face.

"Just where did you come from, little one? Someone drop you off, someone who didn't want you?"

She stood, the puppy in her arms, moving to the edge of the porch, looking around and seeing no one. "I guess I have to make a trip to town, do I, little one? I need to find out who you belong to. At any rate, I need to get food for you, don't I? I don't have anything suitable."

She looked up and frowned, seeing a car approaching her. She sighed. Now, what and who? I really am not in the mood for visitors. Then, conviction came over her. Lord, I really need to work on my attitude towards people, don't I?

She watched as the lady exited the car and stood for a moment looking around before she approached Faith, who had moved down the stairs to stand on the path.

"Good morning. You must be Faith. I'm Seth's mother, Martha. I meant to stop by on Saturday, but time got away from me." She reached to hug Faith, taking her by surprise. "And who do you have here?"

"Welcome, and thank you. I have no idea. She just appeared at my door." Faith looked down at the puppy, now cuddled contentedly in her arms. "I need to find out if she belongs to anyone."

"If she just appeared on your doorstep, then I would say no. I don't recognize her from anyone nearby. I can ask around for you, but this time of year, we get people dropping off puppies they don't want. I would say you have yourself a new friend." She looked up at that, catching a look on the younger woman's face she couldn't read.

Faith had frozen in spot, Martha's voice sounding familiar, and she didn't know why. She didn't remember meeting her before, but she might have. She felt warmed and welcomed by the woman's presence.

"Come in. I've managed to clean the house after it was ransacked. Do you want coffee or tea? At least, I think I have tea. I'm not sure what all Dad packed for me that I tucked away into the cupboards."

Martha laughed as she reached to rub the puppy's ears. "Either will do. Let me help. You have your hands full there."

Later, Martha stood beside the younger woman, her eyes on the garden, but keeping a watch on her face as well.

"You've cleared your grandmother's garden. She was so upset for the last couple of years she wasn't able to get at it, and she refused to let anyone work in it. She would never say why, though." She walked towards the garden, a frown on her face. "Was it just you and Seth?"

Faith nodded, tripping over the puppy at her feet and barely catching herself from falling. "We did. Someone else has been here. Last night, I think." She looked around, chills running through her. "Martha, did you ever see the statue or whatever that was in the centre of the garden? I can't find it and Mom said there was something there."

Martha studied the area, before walking through to stand staring down at the spot. "There was, my dear. A statue of a girl and a dog, not unlike you and your new friend. I wonder what happened to it? It was here six weeks ago." She turned to study the buildings. "Have you looked in the outbuildings?"

Faith shook her head. "Not yet, I haven't. I've been getting the house back in order and the garden, with Seth's help."

Martha smiled, sensing something in Faith's voice. "He said he had been helping a friend. He didn't say the friend was you. I think Joseph suspected and I must admit, so did I. You must come for supper one night, my dear. It would be a pleasure to have a friend's granddaughter in our home."

Faith nodded. "Maybe at some point. Right now, I'm not sure of anything, not even how long I plan to stay here." She turned back to look at the house. "It's in good shape, really, better than I thought on Friday when I got in."

"Your grandmother made sure to keep it up. If you're looking for trades people, talk to Seth. He knows a lot of them."

"What actually does he do, anyway? He never said."

"And he won't. I'll let him tell you. That way, it will make more sense." She shook her head at Faith's questioning look. "No, I won't tell you."

Faith walked her to her car, waving as she drove off, her eyes falling to the puppy now asleep in her arms. "You know, little girl, I'll have to come up with a name for you. Right now, I have to head to town to get you some supplies. Into the pantry with you, for now."

Faith wandered the aisles of the local grocery store, being stopped frequently by townspeople, who welcomed her to town. She frowned finally, staring down at her basket.

"I need to get out of here. This is too much."

"If it's too much, they do credit for you."

She looked up at the deep voice, seeing the grin on Seth's face. She shook a finger at him. "That is not what I meant. I meant that this is too much, all these people stopping me. I shop by myself, not speaking with anyone."

"I'm sure you do in your town, but not here. This is a small town. It seems like everyone knows your business, but that's not the case. It's just they loved your grandmother so much and they want to honour her by making you feel welcome."

She glared at him. "I'm glad she made them all feel so special. Too bad it didn't carry through to family." She brushed by him, her anger evident to him.

He stood, hand to his cheek, wondering again what had caused this anger towards the woman he had known and loved as a grandmother. He ran to catch up with her, finding her driving away. Now, what did he do? He looked around, seeing a car following her, and frowned. His keys in his hand, he ran for his truck, fear in his heart that she would be hurt.

Faith ran for the house, the bags in her hands, dropping them on the kitchen table and then dropping to the floor, her back to the wall, her arms wrapped around her knees. She was afraid, more afraid that she had ever been in her life, and she didn't know why. Lord, what is it about this house, this town? Why am I so afraid? I don't get it. I just want to leave, I don't want to stay here.

She looked up as she heard whining and rose to let the puppy out, scooping her into her arms and hugging her tight before finding the bowl and food she had bought for her. Later, out in the yard, she smiled at the puppy's antics, vaguely hearing a car stop and then approaching footsteps.

"I see you have a new friend." Seth grinned at her as she turned.

"I do. Would you know anything about that?" She suspected he had dropped the puppy off but his look told her differently.

"No, not me. Where did you find her?"

"At my front door." She sighed, feeling the nudge from the Lord. "I'm sorry, Seth. Once again I have to apologize to you. My temper has not improved being here."

"Not that I could tell." He grinned and ducked her playful swat. "I talked to Mom earlier. She asked if we had looked in the outbuildings."

"She did the same to me. And no, I haven't been there." She spun to stare at him. "Why aren't you at work?"

"Because I'm waiting for material." He grinned at her once again. "I'm a landscape artist. I design the gardens for someone else to grow."

She frowned again. "So is that how you knew what to do here?"

He shook his head as he reached to pick up the puppy and then pointed to the nearest shed. "No. I spent a lot of time here with your grandmother. I used to do her yard work."

He paused, his eyes searching around him, feeling what she had, the eyes on them. "Faith, can you take your puppy and head for the house? Please? I'll explain in a moment."

She nodded, turning and running for the house, slamming the door after her and shoving home the bolts. Now what, she thought, eying the window in the door. They can still get in, just by breaking a window. She paced, not knowing what Seth had meant when he asked her to run, the puppy romping around her feet.

Seth moved quickly and quietly towards the nearest shed, having seen movement there. He searched around the outside, and then tried the knob. The door was yanked forward, pulling him with it, his

balance off as he tried to regain his footing.
A sudden blow to the back of the head, and
he was slumped to the floor, unmoving. The
figure peered around the open door and then
ran.

Chapter 5

*R*ubbing at his head, Seth was on his feet, staggering back to the door, his hand reaching out to grasp the frame before he was running for the house, afraid for Faith. He saw no sign of his assailant, but that would be about right, he thought. The trees are close enough, he would be in them and gone before anyone knew what was going on. I need to get Fred over here with his dogs and see if he can track this guy and maybe find something the police can use.

He pounded at the back door, calling for Faith. The door flew open and he staggered through, caught off balance. Her arms were around him to catch him and he hugged her tight.

"You're okay? He didn't get to you?" Seth's voice came in gasps, worry and something else she just didn't understand in it.

"I'm fine." She stared in horror at his head. "You're bleeding. What did he do to you?"

"He hit me from behind when I went into the first building. I think he took off for the woods behind you. I would like to bring in a friend and his dogs, to see if we can track him and maybe stop him. That is, if you agree."

She moved away from him, her hands rubbing up and down her arms, before she reached to pick up the puppy. "I need to name her, Seth. I just don't know what breed she is." Seth knew full well that she was avoiding his question and smiled to himself. He would still bring his friend over to search.

Seth walked over, his hand reaching out to touch the puppy's ears and then stroke her head. "I thought Border Collie first, but now I'm not sure. I would say more Shetland Sheepdog. She has that look. If she's a purebred, someone might be looking for her." He looked up, seeing the sadness in her face at the thought she might not be able to keep her and determined right then and there he would find the owner and purchase the puppy for her.

"Thank you. I just don't know my dog breeds. Not many of them, I mean." She looked down at the puppy eyes looking up at here. "Sara. That's her name. It suits her."

"It does. Here, let me have her for a moment." He gently gathered the puppy into his hands and held her up to look her over. "That's a Sheltie. I have a friend who has one, only hers is a sable. But then I have another friend who has some Shelties as well."

"Sable?" She turned a questioning look at him. "I'm sorry. You lost me."

"Shelties come in more than one colour. There are sables, the brown ones, but there are different shadings or colourings in sable. Then, you have the tricoloured ones, black, white and tan. Then you have the blue merles. They are grey, black, white and tan. The bi-blues are grey and white. And then you have ones like this little girl. Bi-blacks. Black and white. And there are other dilute colourings and double merles, which are white and can have major health issues."

"Wow! I didn't realize there were so many colourings in them. How do we find out about her?"

He handed her Sara and reached for his phone, holding it up. "Let me call Frank and see what he has to say."

He turned back to her when he finished his conversation, pausing as he saw her standing in the light from the window, her head bent over Sara, and thought, I could handle seeing this every day. He stopped. Lord, I have no right to think this. I don't know if she has a boyfriend or not. Guide me here, please.

Faith looked up. "What did he say?"

He shook his head to clear it. "Sara was one of his. Someone purchased her for you. He is sworn to secrecy. He can't tell me who it was, but it was someone who knew you needed a friend."

"Well, isn't that something? Sara, I guess you're stuck with me." She hugged the puppy and then set her down, heading for the door, before she spun. "Your head, Seth. I need to look at it."

"No, you don't. It's fine. The bleeding has stopped and there really isn't a cut at all."

She turned, upset that he wouldn't let her see it, but amused at how he had brushed off her concern. Typical male, she thought, her eyes searching the area. She could still feel the eyes on her.

"Seth, could someone have put up a camera around here? Is that why I feel that I am being watched?"

"That's a good question. It is a possibility but I don't think so." He reached for her hand and tugged her with him. "Come on. I need to show you something. Something that will help you understand your grandmother a little bit better."

She following him, pulling on her hand to get him to release it, but his grip tightened. He paused at the creek, then pointed to an area further down than she ha walked.

"Down there."

He released her hand as they paused, her eyes on the well worn bench that sat there. "Grandmother spent time here?"

"She did. She would say it was her prayer closet. She was one of our prayer warriors."

"I never knew her. I don't remember her. Mom would come and visit, but not bring me. When I was younger, I couldn't understand that. When I grew up, it really didn't matter. She was a relative, but that was all." She looked back at him, seeing the sorrow on his face. "We can't change what happened in the past, Seth. That's not possible."

"I know. She loved you a lot, you should understand that. She prayed constantly for you." He stood, looking out over the water to the hills in the distant, the

46

air fresh and clear for a change. "I'll be down near the path. Come find me when you're ready to go back to the house. Sara, come with me, girl."

Sara looked at her mistress and then scampered after Seth, her tail wagging with pleasure as he reached to scratch her ears.

Faith stood for a moment, her eyes on the bench, before she sat, her hand rubbing along the well-worn wood. Grandmother, I didn't know you. I'm finding out now that I should have. And I have no idea why that was. You wouldn't come and visit. Mom had to come here. Dad and I would stay home when I was younger. Please, can you help me to understand why?

Tears flowed down her face as she raised it in the shadows, to search the sky, looking for answers that weren't there. Lord, I need to understand. Something happened years ago, didn't it? Something that kept me from coming back. I need to know what that was. I need to find out, no matter the cost. I can't go on with my life if I don't. I feel like something is about to break loose and happen, and I'm scared. Please, dear Lord, cover me with Your hand. Shelter me. Help me to find that strong tower that You have prepared for us. Help me to find Your sanctuary.

She finally grasped the front of the seat, then ran her hands along it, stopping as she felt something there. She knelt, her eyes searching for what she had felt. A tug brought loose a small tin box that she turned over and over in her hands, a frown on her face, before she looked up, seeing the writing on the back of the bench for the first time.

She rose, her fingers tracing the letters as she read the words: I do not pray for these alone, but also for those who will believe in Me through their word. John 17:20.

She finally walked away, deep in thought, wonder in her that her Grandmother had spent so much time there the seat was worn and smooth. She looked up and stopped for a moment, seeing Seth standing there, not watching for her, his head raised, his eyes closed. She knew he was lost in prayer and hesitated to disturb him. He turned as he heard a sound and reached out a hand for her, walking her back to the house, not releasing her hand.

She finally spoke. "I found this, Seth. I have no idea what it is. Do you recognize it at all?"

He took the tiny metal box and shook his head. "No, I don't. Did you open it?"

She stared at it. "No. I didn't. I'm not sure if I even want to."

He smiled at her. "Then, let me. It will take a bit to get it open, I think." He was finally able to pry the top of the box.

She leaned against his arm, her hair falling forward until she wrapped a hand around it and held it back. "That a key. But what does it fit?"

"That I'm not sure of. It certainly isn't an ordinary lock. Or even a padlock." He paused, then looked at her, her face so close to his he could see the faint sprinkling of freckles across her nose and cheeks. "It might be a safety deposit box. Do you know if your Grandmother had one?"

She shrugged as she took the key, turning it over and over in her hands. "I don't know. I still have to go to the bank and do that paperwork. Maybe they'll know there."

"Listen, if you would like, I can free up some time tomorrow and take you."

"You would do that? For me? And I haven't been nice to you. At least not all the time."

He laughed at the chagrined look on her face. "I would gladly, Faith. Just let me know what time you want to head in and I'll pick you up."

She watched him walk away, Sara sitting on her foot, yips sounding through the air that her friend had deserted her. Faith laughed and swooped her into her arms, her face against the puppy's head, avoiding the fast moving tongue.

"He'll be back, Sara. He's promised. He'll be back." A sadness suddenly filled her heart, why she had no idea. "And that's what I'm afraid of, Lord. I have no desire to stay in this town, but it seems You have other plans for me. Please, Lord, don't let me fall for him. I have to leave, and I don't want to hurt him.

She paused, her eyes on the garden, a thoughtful look on her face before she sighed and headed for the house. Her internet had been hooked up that day and she needed to see what work was outstanding for her. She was a proofreader and editor for a Christian publishing house and knew there would be books waiting for her.

She paused once more, her eyes now on the path to the creek, and her thoughts turned to the woman she had not known and how her prayers had continued through the years. Lord, she breathed, let me be like that. I can

feel danger closing in, and I have no idea
why. You are here and will protect me. Lord,
I claim that promise, even though I have no
idea what's coming.

Chapter 6

Seth tapped at his steering wheel the next morning, uncertainty filling him. That was unusual for him. He was a confident man, sure of what he wanted and how to go about that, his manner bringing strength and comfort to those around him, his daily walk with God an example for others to follow. Meeting Faith had thrown him off his charted course, he thought, and that was putting it mildly.

He finally pulled into Faith's lane, parked and ran for her door, the gentle rain hitting at his hat as he tugged it down.

Faith stood watching, uncertainty in her movements, as he grinned at her and waited as she locked the door, reaching for her hand and running with her back to his truck, shutting the door of it after before running around and sliding behind the wheel.

"It's raining."

"That it is." He grinned at her again. "Didn't notice before, did you not?"

She shook her head at him, her eyes catching something in the mirror. "Seth, is someone behind us?"

He looked in the rearview mirror. "There is. My Dad. He had to head to the city today, so he's setting out now. He'll be back late tonight." He reached for her hand, squeezing it gently, before his hand was back on the wheel.

He parked, then once more laid a hand on her arm, stopping her as she reached for the door.

"Let me pray first, Faith. We need to walk with God on this. That's what your Grandmother would want."

She paused, her eyes watching the activity on the sidewalk in front of them, before she nodded. "I guess you're right."

Seth bowed his head, his words bring comfort and peace to her troubled heart.

She stood for a moment inside the bank doors, seeing the old-fashioned look of the building but the modern technology that ran it as well. She walked forward to the reception counter, feeling Seth's presence by his hand on her back. A few questions, and they were seated in the manager's office, declining his offer of coffee.

Faith handed over the key. "I found this on Grandmother's property. We're not sure what it belongs to. Perhaps a safety deposit box?"

The manager looked at it, then at her. "That it is. She said she left it somewhere safe, that when the time was right you would find it and come in." He stood. "Come with me. I'll take you to a room you can use. Seth, are you coming as well?"

He nodded, his eyes on Faith's face, and seeing her need and desire for him to be there, but that she would also not ask him to do just that.

He watched as she stood, her hands on the box, nervously biting at her lips.

"Do you want me to open it for you?" He didn't think she did, but had to offer.

She shook her head. "No. I have to do this. I just don't know what I'll find." She reached to unlock the box, her hands hesitating once more before she lifted the lid.

She stopped, her eyes on the papers inside, before she reached for them, pulling them out one at a time, scanning them and setting them aside. She stopped when she saw a sealed envelope, her name written in a hand she recognized.

"She left me a letter, Seth." Her voice was barely audible. "I can't read it here."

"Then, we'll take these with us. Is there anything that needs to remain here?"

She shook her head. "Not really. There are no deeds or anything like that. More just some receipts, notes about things I need to follow up with, and then that letter." She closed the box and gathered up the material, sticking it into her purse. "I'm ready to leave now."

He watched as she walked back towards the manager, who nodded and moved his way.

"Is she okay, Seth? She's not saying much."

"She won't. I'm just beginning to get to know her and she won't say a word about much."

The manager watched the two walk away, his thoughts not on them, but on the man who had approached him, wanting access to that very box, demanding it in fact. He sighed. He was being blackmailed now by that man, but what was in that box was no longer under his care. He hoped the young woman had enough sense not to go around saying she had that paperwork at home. He had no idea what was contained in it, but someone certainly wanted it.

Faith stared down at the papers later. Seth had dropped her off, apologized he couldn't stay, and promised to come back. She idly rubbed Sara's ears as she sat at the table, Sara on her knee, and then moved the papers with a long tanned forefinger.

Grandmother, I have no idea what you were thinking. There are no legal papers here, just receipts for purchases, a receipt for the statue from 20 years ago. She paused. Twenty years? That's about the time she stopped coming to see her. What had happened at that point?

She reached for her phone, scrolling through to her mother's number, and then paused. Should she call her or not? She really needed to hear her mother's voice, but she also didn't want to worry her and that she knew without a shadow of a doubt she would. She jumped as her phone rang, Sara barking wildly as she jumped down and ran in circles before spinning around next to her chair.

"Mom? Hi!" Faith was not surprised to hear her mother's voice. "How are you?"

"Feeling much better, love. And how are you? Working hard on the house?"

"No, not really. Just kind of staring around, trying to figure out where to start."

"Start with the garden, love. That was Mom's favourite place, almost, in the whole world. She would spend hours out there, sometimes just taking a chair and sitting by it, her Bible on her lap."

"We've done that. The garden has been cleared."

"We? Who did you take with you? I thought you planned on going on your own?" Faith's mother, Eva, was surprised and puzzled.

"I am on my own. There's a young. man, a neighbour. He came to help. He said he used to do Grandmother's yardwork."

"Oh, Seth! How nice! Yes, he would be a good help. You say you finished clearing it? When your Dad was down for her funeral, he said it was quite overgrown."

"It was, Mom. Dad never said anything about the house, though, Mom. Why not?"

"I have no idea, love. You'd have to ask him that. I know he and I talked about it. Maybe he thought you were too worried about me to hear much about your inheritance."

"I was, Mom. I was worried. I'm also sorry you couldn't get here for the funeral."

"Me, too, but God had other plans for us, love. Remember how we talked about it, how God has a plan and purpose for us that we don't know about, that we may be a witness to others by His choice and by His chance, and that may have been what His plan was. I certainly didn't intend to fall and end up needing surgery."

"I know you didn't, Mom." Faith paused, sorting through the paperwork until she found the letter. "Grandmother left me a letter."

"Did she? I wondered if she had. Your Dad brought one back for me. I still have to read it. I'm not quite ready to hear her final words. Have you read yours?"

"Not yet. I think I might later today. Seth showed me her prayer bench."

"It's still there? She's had that for so many years. As crippled as she had become, I thought she might have stopped using it."

"She hadn't, Mom. I found a safety deposit box key on the underneath of it yesterday." She rose, pacing as she talked. "Does Grandmother have a safe here?"

"She does. It's behind the picture of your Grandfather in the back parlour. The combination is your birthdate."

"Well, that makes it easy. I have some papers I wanted to put somewhere safely. The house was ransacked the other day, but we don't think they found what they were looking for."

"Oh, my, Faith. Please stay safe. Your grandmother mentioned men wanting to buy her place." She paused. "The statue in the garden. Have you seen it yet? She said she bought it because it reminded her of you and her little collie pup."

"That's the thing, Mom. It's missing. I can see where it was, but it's not there any longer."

"Missing?   Oh, dear.   Have you reported it yet?"

"Not yet. We're planning on searching the out buildings, but haven't had a chance."

"We? As in you and Seth?"

She could hear something in her mother's voice. "Mom? Are you up to something?"

"Never, dear. Not at all. Oh, here's my physiotherapist. I need to run. Once I'm on my feet again, and hopefully that's soon, your Dad and I will be down. If you need him before that, he'll are there."

"I know, Mom. Take it easy on the physio. Love you." She dropped her phone back to the table, her mother's assertion of love for her still ringing in her ears.

"Well, Sara, let's see if the combination does work." She gathered the papers, tucking the letter into her skirt pocket, and headed for the back parlour. She stopped, her eyes looking around, seeing the potential for an office there. Floor-to-ceiling windows lined the corner of two walls and would make a perfect place for her desk, she decided.

As her hand work the safe dial, she paused, realizing what she had just planned. Is this from You, Lord? I know I could work here, but only if it's Your will.

Seth paused in his work, looking up from the blueprints, a sudden chill running down his back. Something was about to break loose, he thought, and it was not a good thing. Lord, protect my lady, he prayed, not realizing he had already claimed her in his heart. Keep her safe. Don't let anyone harm her. He turned as he heard a voice calling to him and walked that way, his mind still on Faith.

She turned as she heard a noise outside and heart pounding, crept to a window, standing back in the shadow so as not to be seen. Sara stayed with her, a low growl coming from the young puppy.

She watched as the two men searched around the garden, arguing she could tell by their body language and their gestures. She breathed a sigh of relief as they left and then ran to her desk, reaching for paper and pen, jotting down their descriptions, their car, and what she could remember of the license plate. She was afraid, more afraid than she had ever felt, except for once. And that one time stayed in the shadows of her mind, not clear at all, but she knew it was from when she was a child.

Chapter 7

$\mathcal{B}$arking wildly, Sara raced through the grass towards the front of the house, leaving Faith standing, hand to her chest, fear racing her through, beside the garden she had been working in. It was late afternoon the next day, and she was not expecting anyone to come and visit her. That she hoped Seth would drop by was an understatement, and she had taken herself to task for that very hope.

Seth jogged towards her, Sara bouncing along beside him, happy to have someone else to play with, she seemed to think. He slid to a stop, his eyes taking in the progress she was making.

"You've been busy." He looked over at her, seeing the sun had been busy on her face as well, bringing out her freckles.

"I've been trying, Seth, but I don't think I've made much progress. I didn't get out here until just a while ago."

"Five or ten minutes here and there, that's all it can take sometimes to make a difference." He shot a look at her again, then to the buildings. "Have you been through the buildings yet?"

She shook her head, wrapping her arms around herself in a defensive manner, her voice full of fear as she spoke. "No. Not after what happened to you." She turned away from him, in an attempt to hide her face and the terror in her eyes. "Besides, there was a car here yesterday, and two men were arguing about the garden."

He stared at her before he moved, his hand coming to rest on her shoulder, and he felt the trembling of her body under his hand.

"Faith? What is it?" He finally turned her to him and when she refused to look up, tilted her chin up with a forefinger. "Look at me, please, Faith. Never be afraid around me. I will do my best to protect you."

She nodded, her eyes finally resting on his face before her gaze sought his, a frown coming to her face as she saw what he was saying with his eyes. His heart stood out in them, and she was not sure she was ready for that kind of complication.

"How was your work today?" Her voice barely above a whisper, she sought to change the subject, to break their locked gaze, anything to keep him from reading her.

He smiled as he let her go, knowing he would come back to that conversation at some point. He pointed towards the nearest building, shed really he thought.

"How about that one, unless you've gotten something else to do?"

She sighed, turning to face the building. "I have some manuscripts waiting to edit and proof, but no, I think we need on that one before we move on." She groaned. "Did I really just say that, committing you to helping when I know you have other places to be?"

He stopped her forward movement with a hand on her arm, waiting until she turned and looked up at him.

He smiled, the smile lighting up his eyes with a look meant only for her. He hadn't acknowledged it yet to himself, but he was falling in love with this lady, had been since she first spit at him in anger. He prayed that she would return his love, but left it with God. He knew best, Seth decided.

"I am only too happy to help you. You can't do this on your own, and so far, I don't see anyone else stepping in. Your safety is important to me. Not just because of your Grandmother, whom I adored, by the way."

She nodded, moving forward and breaking contact with him, not quite sure what he was meaning, but a faint hope and softening filled her heart. Was God working a miracle in her, she wondered? An old boyfriend had told her she had a cold heart, that she would never find anyone to love, she was too unlovable herself. That had hurt and chased away a hope she had had since a child, of being a wife and mother. Suddenly, she determined that boy, really, not a man, would not rule her thoughts and emotions or life any more.

She stood in the shed, turning slowly to observe what was there. "There's really not much here, is there? I thought there'd be more."

"No, not a lot. Mostly just the gardening tools, seeing as it's the closest to the garden." He moved around the shed, searching, pulling tools away from the wall and setting them neatly back, his eyes running up and down the walls, searching for anything that was out of place. "I'm not seeing anything yet, are you?"

She shook her head. "No, but I know something is in here. It seems my Grandmother loved puzzles and secrets. At least, that's what my Mom is now telling me."

Seth started to laugh, causing her to spin and stare at him, thinking he had lost his mind.

"It's okay, Faith. It's just so your Grandmother, what your mother said. She used to come up with scavenger hunts for the youth in the church, and they were always wonderful. Just difficult enough to be challenging but easy enough that anyone could follow them." He paused, his eyes lighting on her.

"Do you think this is what she has planned, then? Sending me on a scavenger hunt to find the statue? What would be the purpose?"

He shrugged, his eyes on the wall behind her, moving past her to touch a spot. "She may well have. Look, this is different than the other wood. It's….It's…."

"Well, I must say, you're real definite there, Mr. Logan." She laughed at the face he made, shoving him aside with her shoulder, and reaching for the spot, her fingers pressing against the wood until she heard a faint click and the wood sprang away from the board it was inserted into. Faith reached into the crevice, pulling out another key and a note. "Looks as if you were right, after all."

He read over her shoulder. "This does not make sense. I have no idea what she would mean by that."

Faith read aloud. "If you search with all your heart and mind, you will find the treasure you seek. It is not where you expect it to be. Search for the unexpected and find the next clue.

"No, it really doesn't. I wonder what she meant."

Seth shrugged. "I would suggest we set it aside for the night. I need to run. I have to be on site very early tomorrow morning." He caught her hand, tucking it into his elbow, as they walked back to the house, their voices quiet in the growing twilight.

He made sure she locked up before he left, his eyes searching what he could around the house, feeling danger still near her, and not seeing where it was. Lord, protect her this night. He didn't realize how much she would need that protection in the next twenty-four hours, and how it would affect their relationship.

Chapter 8

The next morning, Faith immersed herself into her work, rising only when Sara stood up and patted her knee with one front paw. She was growing daily, now coming into the gangly stage. She loved her mistress, that was evident.

"You need out, do you, girl? All right. Just let me grab some juice and we'll head out. I want to see what's coming up in the garden. This is truly an adventure, isn't it?" She laughed as she walked through the door, the pup in such a hurry she tumbled down the stairs, laying still for a moment before rising, shaking herself off and running towards the garden. "You really do understand words, don't you?"

Faith stood, her eyes on the garden, but her thoughts on the paper they had found the night before.

She looked up, startled at the low, throaty rumble of an engine, fear suddenly filling her whole being. She spun, not sure where it was coming from, screaming for

68

Sara as the puppy charged towards the woods. She ran after her, not quite reaching her before a large ATV emerged from the woods. It stopped for a moment, the rider seeming to eye her, but she couldn't tell for sure, not with the full face mask on his helmet. Camouflage clothing covered his body and she could find nothing outstanding about anything. He pointed at her and then the machine was revved, and started into motion, aiming directly for her.

She screamed and turned, running for safety, being cut off from the house and the buildings. She tried to run for the woods, but the machine was there once more. She spun, her breath in gasps, her heart pounding, fear the only emotion she felt. She ran for the creek, but was cut off from there. She slid to a stop, not knowing where to turn next.

Her heart pounding, she stepped backwards, the machine inching forward. She felt wood under her foot and wondered what she had touched. As her other foot stepped up, there was a cracking sound. A scream ripped through the air as the weathered wood split under her weight and she fell, her scream abruptly cutting off as she landed at the bottom of the dry cistern, her head thudding loud through the sudden silence, the dirt and debris that had fallen in through the cracks in the wood somewhat providing a cushion. The man cut the machine motor and walked over to stare down at her, before laughing in a cruel coarse manner, walking back to his machine and riding away. He had accomplished what he wanted, he thought. There was no way she would have survived that, even though it was not a deep cistern.

Hours later, Seth parked, his eyes searching for Faith and not seeing her. He strode towards the house, stopping as he heard the yipping of Sara and then turned to walk around the house, meeting Sara running towards him. He finally managed to corral her against his legs and pick her up.

He frowned, his eyes searching, not seeing Faith. "Where is she, girl? It's not like her to leave you out here on your own. Is she in the house? Shall we go see?"

He walked up to the back door, tapped and then opened it, not seeing Faith. He called for her, not hearing an answer. Fear suddenly hit him. He strode to the pantry, making sure Sara had food and water and closing her in there. He walks rapidly through the downstairs and then hesitated, one foot on the stairs, a hand grasping the worn banister, his gaze on the landing at the top of the stairs. He felt like an intruder but knew he had to make sure she wasn't here.

Standing outside once more, he searched, still not seeing her. He almost ran for the buildings, searching each one and then running for the creek and the prayer bench. Where is she, Lord? She wouldn't go off on her own and leave Sara outside. That's not her.

He slowly walked back towards the house, his eyes on the ground. He stopped and stoopped, his fingers tracing the track of the ATV and fear rose once more.

He spun in a circle again, his eyes on the trees and headed that way, just catching his balance as he walked towards the cistern. His eyes dropped and he saw the splintered wood. No, Lord, please. Not that. Don't let her be down there. He dropped to his knees, carefully leaning over, his heart dropping as he saw the crumpled form at the bottom. She didn't respond to his calls for her to move, to talk to him.

He rose, searching for something to get him down there, and ran for a shed, knowing there was a ladder there.

His phone chiming stopped him in his tracks on his way back with the ladder. He tugged it out of his pocket, frantic to get back to Faith.

"Dad?"

"Son, where are you? Your Mom was expecting you and said you hadn't called yet to say you'd be late."

"I'm sorry, Dad. I stopped by at Faith's and found Sara outside on her own. We need the police and paramedics. It looks as if someone on an ATV went after Faith. I've her at the bottom of the old cistern. I'm just on my way down there now."

"Leave your phone on speaker. We're on our way. Any updates, your Mom will send on."

Seth didn't bother responding, instead sliding the ladder into the cistern, and rapidly sliding down it. He didn't know afterwards if his feet even touched any of the rungs. He dropped to his knees, a shaking hand reaching for her back, his head dropping in relief. She was alive. He knew better than to try and move her, instead his hand coming out to brush back her hair.

Please, Lord, don't let her die on me. I don't know if I can lose a friend I've just made. Protect her and heal her. Please, Lord. I just know she's here for a reason, at her grandmother's house, and that reason she hasn't found yet. At least, I don't think she has, has she, Lord? She might have last night or today.

He heard his father's shouts, and called to him, pocketing his phone as he did so. He looked up to see Joseph heading down the ladder, his mother standing at the top, a hand to her mouth.

"How is she, son?"

"I'm not sure, Dad. She's alive, but I don't know what happened. I think she was chased here. There are a lot of ATV tracks up there."

"I saw that." He turned as he heard the sirens. "Up you go, son. Bring them back here. I'll stay with her until they're ready to transport."

Seth stood at the edge of the cistern, his arm around his mother, hers around him, as the paramedics worked on Faith, assessing her, moving her cautiously to a backboard, a neck collar in place, foam blocks holding her head from moving. He stepped back as she was raised to the surface and to a stretcher, watching as they continued to work on her.

Please, Lord, was his cry. Save her.

He heard the conversations around him as the local police force worked out what they thought had happened, but he didn't pay enough attention to catch their words. He moved forward, his eyes on her face, then reaching for her hand as she moved it restlessly. Her grip tightened on his and he could not remove his hand. He looked up in consternation as the paramedics and firefighters moved to wheel the stretcher to the waiting ambulance.

He finally extricated his hand, standing watching as the ambulance headed out, lights flashing, one of the police cruisers racing ahead of it. He turned as he heard his father speak.

"Come on, son. Let's follow them. She needs someone there. Your Mom is tracking down her father and letting him know, but she's having trouble doing that. They tell her he's been in a meeting and is now on the road home, and that he never answers his phone when he's driving. She'll collect Sara and what she needs and lock up for Faith."

Seth sat, watching closely as the people moved through the Emergency Department waiting room, knowing he would not find about Faith, no matter how much he wanted to. He wasn't family, and they were really strict about that. He looked up in surprise as his name was called. He stood and walked towards the nurse, a puzzled look on his face.

"Seth, come on. The doctor wants to talk to you. We've had permission from her mother to let you know what's going on. I understand you're a good friend of the family."

"I was of her grandmother. She's Mrs. Gordon's granddaughter."

"That's who she looks like. I couldn't place her." She pushed back a curtain to a cubicle. "Here you go. The doctor will be with you shortly."

Seth nodded, his thanks whispering through the air, before he walked towards the stretcher. He didn't look at anything but her face, seeing the faint bruise on her forehead, the scratches on her face. Please, Lord, was all he could pray, but it was enough, he knew. God knew what his prayer was and would answer, as He always did.

He heard someone beside him and turned, seeing the physician there, his eyes on her chart before he moved to assess her once more.

"Seth? Her mother called. She gave us permission to talk to you and your parents. She said her father was on his way but it would take a couple of hours to get here. She's faxed through authorization papers if we need them, but I don't think we will." He studied the chart again, before tucking it under his arm, and leaning against the bed. "She's remarkably lucky. A much deeper hole would have been likely deadly for her. The debris on the bottom helped cushion her fall to some extent seeing that it was not packed tightly on top, being from the last winter or so."

Seth nodded, wondering where the physician was headed with his comments. "How badly is she hurt?"

"A lot of bruising. A concussion for sure. That we know. A sprained ankle she'll need to stay off. A couple of broken fingers. All in all, someone was looking after her today."

"God was, doctor. God was."

The physician shot him a look, shaking his head. He didn't believe, but after today, it might just be worth looking into. "We're moving her to a room shortly. You can stay with her for now."

He walked away, Seth staring after him, before he turned back to the stretcher, his hand reaching for hers, a prayer raising in his heart for healing and for thanksgiving.

God had protected her, he thought, once again. God was faithful.

Late that night, Faith stirred, not quite sure where she was, but knowing she wasn't at home. She couldn't feel the weight of Sara against her legs and that worried her. Her eyes shot open and then just as abruptly closed against the low light on in her room. She left a hand on hers and gripped it tightly. She had no idea where she was, but she was not alone.

Seth moved his chair closer to the bed. He had not left, not wanting to leave her on her own. He knew he would have to soon. Visiting hours were over, but the nursing staff had been lenient with him.

He reached for her hand, hers tightening on his as she tried to open her eyes once more. He watched as her eyes opened once more and she tried to focus.

"Faith?" His voice was low, not wanting to disturb her if she wasn't really awake.

She turned her head, a frown on her face, blinking in an attempt to clear her vision. "Seth? Where am I?"

"You're in the hospital. You had an accident?"

"An accident? What?" She suddenly sat up. "I'm going to be sick."

He reached for the basin the nurses had left, his arm supporting her as she was indeed sick. He removed the basin, rinsing it out and setting it back on the table before he reached for a cloth, wrung it out in warm water, and walked back, the warmth and dampness soothing on her face. She sat up again, and he reached an arm to support her.

"Seth? What happened?" She was still having trouble seeing. "Why are there two of you at times?"

"A concussion, sweetheart. You have a concussion. I won't go into a lot of details, but you fell into an old dry cistern and knocked yourself out, broke a finger or two and sprained an ankle."

She laid back on him, suddenly too tired to stay upright. "I did all that? I don't remember."

He removed his arm and she snuggled back down into the bed, turning to her side, and pulling the blankets up around her neck.

"Will you stay please? I don't want to be alone. I'm scared, Seth, and I don't know why."

Neither of them saw the man hesitating at the door, his hate-filled eyes on Faith. He thought he had finished the task, but now he knew he hadn't. He would try again and be successful next time.

Seth's head turned briefly as he heard a sound and watched the door, not seeing anything there, before he turned back to Faith, seeing her eyes on him. "I can stay for a while, but they might make me leave. Your father's on his way. I thought he would have been here by now."

She sighed. "Not if he was in meetings. They take priority at times with him. Mom and I can come last and have many times." She reached for his hand again, her cold in his warm one. "Thank you. But what about Sara?"

"Mom has her. She picked her up and took her home. She also locked up your home for you."

"Thank her for me, will you?" She yawned. "I'm tired. I think I'll sleep for a while. Please, don't leave me. You'll be here when I wake up? Please?"

"If I can, I will be. I promise." He watched as her eyes closed, before he bent over and kissed the bruise on her forehead. He didn't seen the older man who hesitated in the doorway, his eyes on his daughter and then the young man bending over her.

His steps caused Seth to straighten and spin, ready to defend Faith. Seth paused, his eyes on the man as he stopped, a smile on his face.

"I'm Faith's father, Paul. Thank you for being here. You must be Seith?"

"I am. I don't think we've met for years. I tried to get to speak with you at the funeral but didn't find a chance."

Paul reached to shake Seth's hand. "That's okay. Her mother and I appreciate that you stayed with her. I tried to get here as soon as I could, once her mom reached me. Traffic was backed up from a large accident and I had to detour around it. That took a few more hours than I planned." He reached to touch his daughter's face, to drop a kiss on her cheek. "What have they said?"

"A concussion, bruising, a couple of broken fingers, a sprained ankle. All in all, it could have been a lot worse."

Paul nodded, his eyes on the young man, sensing something more. "What aren't you saying, Seth?"

Seth nodded towards the hall. "Can we talk out there? She's just managed to get back to sleep. She's been having double vision and was sick a while ago."

"Not a problem. You seem to care deeply for her." Paul shook his head at Seth's look. Does he not realize, Lord, that he's in love with my daughter? Is that why You brought her here? To find that one love You prepared for her? If so, then we'll have to let her go. She's been moving that way for months now. She's not been content in our town.

"Seth? What is it?" Paul stood, hands in his jacket pocket, watching the younger man as he sorted through his thoughts.

"How much do you know about her grandmother's garden? Do you remember the statue that was there?"

Paul's eyes were shuttered as he nodded. "I do. And I remember the reason for it. That's something I have to talk to Faith about, and I am not looking forward to that conversation."

Seth waited for him to continue, but when he didn't, looked around, seeing the movement of the nursing staff, his eyes catching sight of a man just disappearing around the corner, thinking vaguely that he knew him, but shook his head. That man had left town a few years ago and never been back, swearing he was shaking the dust of the town off his feet. Seth had never really heard what had happened.

"Then, I hate to tell you. It's missing. I don't know if you had noticed at the funeral or not. Faith found the marks and we've started searching for it, but so far haven't had a chance to go through many of the buildings." He paused, not quite sure how to tell a father his daughter was in danger, that today had not been an accident.

Paul sighed. "You're telling me today wasn't a chance accident, then? Is that what you're afraid to say? I figured that one out when the police called me, asking me for details on Faith's life and if she had any enemies. That conversation occurred on my way here and took a long time. That's part of the reason I was delayed."

Seth nodded. "She's had issues since the day she arrived. I gather she has said nothing to you. It sounds just like her. I found her unconscious the night she arrived. She's found footprints around the property in the morning, from men wandering around at night. I'm working on a security system for her, but she's resisting that." He paused, a slight grin on his face. "She's stubborn, that one. And someone provided a puppy for her."

"A puppy, is it? Now that is a wonder. She doesn't like dogs, hasn't since she was a child."

Seth waited but Paul didn't continue, turning instead to face his daughter's room. "I'll stay for a while. I can't thank you enough for what you've done, Seth." He paused, not quite sure how to ask what he needed. "I have a conference call tomorrow morning I have tried everything to get out of but circumstances with us all mean it has to go ahead. I don't want that. I want to be with my daughter. Is it too much to ask if you could spare some time to be with her?"

"I will be here. What time?"

Chapter 9

Glaring at the wall, Faith waited, for what she wasn't quite sure. She just knew someone was to take her home and they weren't there. Her father had been there, they had talked well into the morning, before he apologized, said he had to take that call, had tried his best to get out of it but had had to leave. She had expected that, she thought, not wanting to be on her own. She refused to look up as the door opened and footsteps approached.

Seth waited, a grin on his face, knowing that Faith was aware someone was there, but determined to ignore them.

"Faith, it won't work." He finally spoke.

She shot him a look, eyes narrowed. "What won't?"

"Ignoring me. I'm here to spring you. I let your Dad know I was here to take you home." He waited for her to speak. "Did you not understand? You can leave. They want your bed for someone who is really sick."

"Very funny. I can really leave?"
Hope sprang into her eyes. She hated
hospitals, always had and had received no
explanation as to why. She just knew her
parents knew but they didn't tell her or
wouldn't tell her.

"You can. The nurse is on her way to
help you get ready. I have a wheelchair
outside your door with your name on it."

She shook her head at him just as he
turned to leave. She reached for his arm,
stopping his movement, bringing his eyes to
hers, a frown on his face as he saw something
there.

"Thank you. Dad said you stayed with
me all afternoon and evening, until he got
here. He explained about the police and the
traffic. That I can understand."

Seth watched the changing expressions
on her face, not wanting to break contact with
her. He fought against the feeling he had, that
somehow their lives were entwined more
than just from today, and he couldn't place
why.

"You're more than welcome, Faith.
I'm glad to be here for a friend. It's who I
am. Now, let me get the nurse for you."

She refused to let go of him, instead reaching to pull his face down and placing a kiss on his cheek, surprising both of them. She blushed, looking everywhere else but at him, and missing the tender look he had for her.

The nurse bustled in at that moment and Seth stepped away, leaning against the wall outside her door. He frowned as he watched a man pacing near the waiting room, his eyes on Faith's room every time he turned that way. Seth still felt that he knew him, but the name still eluded him. He looked around as he heard the door open and saw the nurse reach for the wheelchair, pushing himself away from the wall and heading back to Faith. Lord, heal my friend. Help us to find out who it was that did this to her.

Faith settled down on her couch, Sara jumping up to lick at her face, causing giggles to come from her, before the puppy settled down on her knee, content to have her mistress with her once more. Seth's mom was there, fixing Faith a meal, watching closely how Seth tenderly cared for her.

Lord, I have no idea what's going on here, but You do. Protect their hearts. I can see they falling in love and then Faith heading back for town, leaving Seth here.

Seth stepped away from her, with a word for his mother, before he headed outside. Paul was there, waiting for him, ready to walk the property

"I thought the cistern was well covered." Paul frowned, thinking of how he daughter had been hurt.

"It was. I noticed that the other night when we walked back past it from the creek. It has to have been uncovered since then. Faith wouldn't have known where it was. We never talked about it."

"No, she wouldn't. Let's take a look." Paul stood for a moment, a frown once more on his face.

Seth headed down the ladder, his eyes on the wood. He froze as he held up a piece, passing it up to Paul.

"Take a look at that, Paul." Paul had insisted that Seth call him by his first name, not Mr. Webster.

"What am I looking at, Seth? I'm not good with wood."

"Take a look at the end that broke." Seth searched for more, stopping for a moment as he heard the sound of an exclamation from Paul and stepping back so he could look up at him.

"It was cut, Seth. Sabotaged. This was not just a chance accident. It was planned." Paul could feel the anger rising in him and wanted to hit out at someone, something, anything.

"That's my take. I'm sure the police have made the same decision." Seth turned as he heard a metal sound as he moved his foot, and reached down, finding another small metal tin. "What's this?"

"What did you say?" Paul peeked over the edge, watchful as Seth tucked the box into his pocket and then climbed back out.

"I found another box for Faith. It would appear her Grandmother has sent her on a scavenger hunt of sorts. But I don't think she would have arranged this. I think the box was likely on the pile of wood and fell down when it broke under her."

Paul nodded. "More than likely you're correct." He grinned suddenly. "A scavenger hunt? You know, she loved those. Said they made her think of the fun she and her siblings and friends had had as children with them." He started to laugh, bringing Seth's eyes to him as they walked back towards the house. "I can remember the night I came out here to talk to her grandfather, to ask for her Mom's hand in marriage. Her

88

grandmother sent me on a scavenger hunt to find her. That's a memory we've cherished all these years."

"Now that sounds like something she'd do. Do you plan on doing that with Faith?" Seth grinned as Paul stopped, a shocked look on his face.

"Now, that I never thought of. Thank you for the idea, Seth."

"What idea?" Faith stood in the kitchen, her eyes on the two men.

"Your dad mentioned your grandmother sent him on a scavenger hunt to find your mother the night they got engaged. I think I just suggested he do the same with you."

She stared at him, her mouth open before she snapped it closed, her eyes narrowing at the grin her father was trying hard to hide. "He wouldn't dare."

"Don't dare a man, dear. They take that as a challenge." Martha patted her on the shoulder. "Now, sit. You're not supposed to be walking on that ankle."

Faith dropped into a chair, her eyes still on her father as he struggled to control his laughter. "Dad?"

"Don't worry, love. Would I do that to you?" He dropped a kiss on her hair as he walked past her to wash up for the meal, her mutter that's exactly what he would do, causing him to break out into fresh laughter.

Seth slid into a chair beside her. "How are you feeling now?"

She shrugged. "Sore, and in a bad mood. I hate being sick."

Seth began to laugh. "Really? I would never have guessed." He waited until the meal was finished before he pulled out the box. "I found one of these in the cistern. I suspect it was on the wood and ended up down there when you did."

She poked at it. "I don't want to open it, Seth. Look at what happened with the first one."

He nodded. "I know that. But that was not your doing, now was it? I would never have thought of looking there, which is what I think your Grandmother meant. Now, open this one."

She shoved it back towards him. "You do it. I'm not touching it." She missed the laughing looks the two older people exchanged.

"Are you sure? Because once I open it, you can't, you know?"

"How on earth did you ever make it through college? Your deduction skills are atrocious."

Seth began to laugh harder at that, finally seeing the smirk she gave him. "I made it through very well, thank you. I didn't have to use my deduction skills. That's why they are rusty."

He reached for the box, working to remove the lid, finding a folded piece of paper as well as a small object. He frowned at the object, not sure what it was.

His mother reached for it. "I have not see one of these in years. It's an old brooch, Seth. It was popular when your grandparents were young. Now, why would she hide that?"

"Mom Gordon had a strange sense of humour at times. She was a wonderful woman, don't get me wrong, but she could certainly have you going, as they say." Paul studied the brooch, before he looked up at the two younger people, who sat, heads close together, studying the note. "What does it say?"

"Not much, I'm afraid." Seth sat back, frustrated.

Faith began to read. "Riches are not the end of life. Wisdom and love are. When you find the right jewel, then you find both."

"I have no idea what she meant. Do you, Faith?" Seth reached for the brooch, studying it, a frown on his face.

"No, and I don't want to. I do not want another adventure, thank you very much."

Paul shook his head at the way the younger couple were squabbling, seeing Martha trying hard to hide her own laughter.

"Let's put this up for the night, then, shall we? Martha tells me she needs to leave soon. I want to talk a walk down to Mom's prayer bench. I need some time there. Seth, you're staying for a while?"

Seth hadn't looked up from the note as Paul spoke, his mind on the words. "What had she meant?"

Faith shook her head, heading for the living room, Sara scampering along with her. She would let Seth work at that. She just wanted to lay down.

Chapter 10

The next morning, Faith hobbled through the yard, intent on making it to the garden, Sara run circles around her before heading off to sniff, coming running back to check on her and then off again. She laughed at the antics of the puppy, wondering again why she had feared and hated and disliked dogs so much.

She stopped, seeing the new growth in the garden. It was now late spring, she realized, wondering where time had gone. She rested her hand on the cane she was using, refusing the crutches she had been told to use. Crutches and the puppy just didn't mix, she thought.

She wished for a bench near the garden, and turned, a frown on her face. A vague memory had her looking around, knowing that at one time there had been one there.

Paul watched from the porch as she looked around, heading her way at last. He has spoke with Eva, and she was planning on heading that way. Her physiotherapist had released her at last and a friend had offered to make the two-hour drive with her. He was glad of that. He had arranged his own work so that he could here, as much as he could. He didn't like the fact that Faith seemed to have attracted danger of some kind.

"What are you looking for, Faith?"

She jumped before she turned, taking the cup of coffee her father held out for her. "I would love to have a bench here. Wasn't there one at some point? A memory keeps tugging at me, that there was one. That Grandmother had one here. A contemplation bench, wasn't it?"

Paul froze, knowing that the memories Faith had suppressed all those years were finally working their way to the surface. He was glad, wasn't he, Lord, that they were? Wouldn't that help her heal? But he was also afraid, knowing how the memories would hurt.

"She did. I'm surprised you could even remember it. It's been that many years." He handed her his own mug. "Here, hold this for a moment. I know there are some chairs in one of the sheds. I'll get some and you can tell me how to arrange them." He paused. "I have some good news, though. I talked to your Mom."

Faith spun to stare at him, hope alive on her face. "She's coming down? She's done her treatments?"

"She is and yes, she's done. Sally said she'd bring her down either today or tomorrow."

"Oh, that's wonderful." Then, Faith's face clouded, knowing her father would be off to work. "But you have to go back, don't you?"

He shook his head, a gentle smile on his face, even as he reached to hug her, mindful of the two mugs she held. "No, actually, I don't. I have asked for a leave of absence. My vacation has not been used much lately, and you know that. Every time we've planned, something has come up, either with your Mom, or you. Work has had that too. Seeing you in that hospital bed, Faith, made me realize that work had begun to encroach on our family time, more than what any of us want. You'll soon marry and start a family of your own, God willing. I would like to take some time just for us." And Seth, he added silently to himself, if he was reading the younger man correctly.

Faith watched as her father walked away, not moving until Sara nudged her foot. She looked down, then bent, taking the piece of wood from her mouth. She frowned. Now, this looked familiar but why.

Seth wandered up to her about an hour later, dropping into the other chair, his head going back and his eyes sliding closed. He had had a rough couple of days at work, and knew he was exhausted and should be at home but wanting to spend time with Faith.

"Seth. You don't have to come in every day, you know." Faith's voice held a touch of amusement.

He smiled. "But I want to, Faith. I like being around you." He rolled his head enough that he could watch her and saw the conflicting emotions on her face. Please, Lord, I think I'm falling in love with this lady, and do not want to hurt her.

"Yeah, right. Have you had any thoughts on the other note?"

He nodded. "I do. There's a board in the second shed that looks like a cut jewel. Your Grandmother had made sure that it stayed in place, how I can't tell. Glue, nails, whatever it took."

"Can we go take a look at it? I'm ready to get on with the hunt and get it over with." Faith stood, reaching for her cane, surprised when his hand came out and he waited for her. "Seth?"

"I don't bite, you know. This is easier." He clasped her hand in his and together they walked towards the second shed, not much bigger than the first one.

Faith stood, watching the dust motes dance in the sunlight, before she turned in a circle, her hand coming out to his arm to balance herself. "Where is it, Seth? This shed seems empty."

"She emptied it last year. It had a bunch of old equipment in it that she sold off. This way." He led her towards the back corner, his finger coming out to trace the diamond-shaped knot. "This is it."

"But why would she direct us here?"

"That's an interesting question." Seth searched the shed, then walked outside and around to the back, searching as he walked, finally stopping at the knot and looking up. "Found it, Faith."

She leaned against him, her hand on his back, as she too looked up. "Up there. I can see it. Can you reach it?"

"I can. Let me just stand on this stump." He was as good as his word, balancing carefully, her hand on his waist, as he reached for the eaves and gently worked loose another tin box, stepping down. He looked at her, catching a look on her face, that had him wondering what her thoughts were.

"How did she get that up there?" Faith was puzzled, knowing her grandmother had been frail that last winter.

"I think she had such a determination to set this up for you, that she just did it. I can't be certain though. I didn't see her doing this, but I'm sure we have another clue to follow."

She turned as she heard voices, fear suddenly on her face. Seth caught her hand and pulled her along the far side of the shed.

"I can't run, Seth. What are we to do?"

He shook his head. "Wait. See what they want."

They listened to the men arguing, their eyes on each other, a shocked look on Seth's face, fear on Faith's. He laid a finger on her mouth to stop her words and then cautiously led her to the next shed and then the next one, moving her further away from the men.

"Seth? What's going on?" Faith's fear was overcoming her and she began to shake.

"I know that voice, but I didn't think he was still around." He leaned back against the wooden wall of the barn, gathering his thoughts even as he tried to breath easily. "Are you okay? You shouldn't be running on that ankle."

"Who cares? What is going on?" She bit back more words as they heard the men approaching and Seth once more grabbed her hand, leading her towards a pile of wood covered by a tarp. He lifted a corner, shoved her underneath the tarp and then crawled in after her, pulling the tarp back down over them. He reached an arm to pull her tight to him.

She buried her head against his shoulder, fear causing her body to shake. Please, Lord, don't let them find us.

Seth listened, hearing the men walk away, and still waited. They finally heard someone approach, calling for them.

"Faith, hon, come on out. It's safe now, hon. Where are you?"

Faith started, a frown on her face as she looked up at Seth in the dimness. It sounded like her father, but he would never call her hon. That was a given. He would call her love, not hon. Seth looked down at her, a question on his face. It sounded like Paul, but Faith wasn't moving, so he stayed right with her. They finally heard footsteps moving away.

Faith leaned close to Seth's ear. "That wasn't Dad. He would never call me hon."

"It sounded like him. Are you sure?"

She nodded. "I am absolutely sure. Dad doesn't like that short form. He would never use it." She sat, lost in thought, before he moved. She clutched at his arm. "Is is safe?"

"Let me slip out and see if we can get back to the house. I have a feeling they've moved on. Here, hold on to this." He slipped her the tin box before he studied her face, a decision forming in his mind, acting on it before he could stop himself. He reached and kissed her, then moved the tarp aside, his eyes alert, his movements as quiet as he could make them.

He tucked the tarp back down around the wood, praying that the men had indeed gone and that he could bring Faith back to the house in safety. He edged around the buildings, eyes watchful, listening for any sound from the men. He finally gave a sigh of relief. They were alone.

He turned to head back for Faith, his eyes dropping to the ground. What was that, he wondered? He stooped, picking up the object, turning it over in his hand. It wasn't something he recognized. Shrugging, he stuffed it into a pocket and headed for Faith.

She blinked in the sudden sunlight as Seth reached to help her out, the pain in her ankle causing her to stumble. She gave a low cry as he swept her into his arms after he had tucked the tarp back and then headed for the house.

"Seth! Put me down! Right not!" Faith struggled to get free, to stand on her feet.

Seth looked down at her and shook her head, an unreadable look on his face. "Sorry, Faith. I've just pulled you all over the back forty, as they say, and that ankle has to hurt. Just lie still and I'll set you down as soon as we get back to the house. See? Sara's waiting for you at the door. This is the quickest way to get there."

She finally subsided in her struggles, not happy with him at all. He waited as she opened the door and then gently shoved it shut with his heel once they were in the kitchen, heading for the living room.

She sat up on the couch, not at all happy with him, but knowing he had been right.

Lord, I really do need to work on my attitude, don't I? Help me in that, please.

Seth moved away, setting the box on the coffee table, and then reaching down to pick up Sara, heading for her food bowl and then setting coffee for the two of them. He knew Paul had arranged to meet Eva in a town about thirty minutes away and wouldn't be back for a while yet.

Faith sighed, knowing she'd have to apologize yet again. She heard Seth's gentle voice, heading out with Sara and then back in, finally heading her way, his voice calm and gentle with the growing puppy. He set her coffee beside her and then sat, his hand reaching for the box, turning it over and over, not speaking.

"Are you going to open that?" Faith's voice was subdued, not at all like her.

He shrugged, before reaching for her hand and dropping the box into it. "Your Grandmother seemed to think you needed this. You should open it." He stared at her for a moment, seeing the contriteness she was feeling. He sighed. How did he approach her now?

Faith finally spoke. "Those men, Seth. Do you know them?"

"One of them. He's the brother of a friend of mine. I thought he had left the area years ago, but it seems as if he's back. I find that strange, that's he back so soon after you Grandmother died. She was instrumental in having him charged in a number of break-ins and thefts."

"His voice sounded familiar, as if I know him. But I don't know how."

"Maybe when you were young, and were here? He was around here with his brother, but your grandparents never really liked or trusted him." He stared down at his mug, sipped from it and then set it back, reaching for her hands. "I need to apologize, Faith. I shouldn't have just picked you up like that. You were right to protest. I guess I was just thinking of getting you out of the area and to safety."

Her hands tightened on his. "I need to apologize too, Seth. You were thinking of just that, and I caused a scene. Had the men still be there, we would have been in trouble. I've been so used to being on my own and not having to consider someone else, that I just reacted negatively. I have to learn not to do that. That's something God has been working on for the last few months. Perhaps that part of the reason I'm here, to learn I have to depend on others, not just myself."

Seth nodded, his eyes still on hers, feeling hope that maybe things would work out for them. "Apology accepted. Just know that I would never do anything to hurt you. Not intentionally, that is. I would give my life to protect someone close to me." He left it at that, reaching for the tin box, not catching the thoughtful look that filled her face or the hope in her eyes.

"What say we try and open this?" He held up the tin. "Your Grandmother had quite the supply of these."

"I know." Faith spoke grumpily, feeling tired and ready to sleep, but it was only late afternoon. "I'm sorry, once again. You didn't deserve that attitude. So, go ahead. I'll let you have the pleasure."

"Pleasure? Is that what it was?" He grinned as she playfully shoved him, Sara barking at them, then scrambling up to lick at their faces, before settling down, a chin on Faith and a paw on Seth.

Seth looked down at her and grinned. "I'd say she's staked her territory, hasn't she?" He had grown to adore the puppy and hated to think of Faith moving back to town and taking Sara with her.

He turned his attention to the box, finding this one easier to take apart, and he frowned. Why was that? He examined it closely, realizing that while there was rust on it, it had been more protected. He lifted the lid and paused, his fingers in midair where he had stopped his hand.

Faith looked at him. "Seth? What is it?"

He shook his head. "I'm not sure. There's a picture, an old one at that. I don't see a note though." He lifted out the photo, handing it to Faith, and then studying the box. He lifted his head to stare at her as she exclaimed, both wonder and pain in her voice.

"Faith? What is it?" He reached to wrap an arm around her, she was that upset.

"This? This photo? It's me. I'm about two, I think, or three at the most. What is going on, Seth? Why would she put this photo there? Is there anything else in the box?"

He shook his head. "Nothing. Is there anything on the back of the photo?"

She turned it over, a frown on her face. "No. It's just the photo. What is so important about it?"

Seth reached for it, his eyes on her face first, seeing the distress there and silently asking God to help her, to calm her, to bring her peace.

He studied the photo, a frown in place. "This is here, out front on the porch I think. Man, it's changed though." He looked again. "Wait. I know that planter. She still has it. It's out front." He was on his feet, pulling Faith up, disturbing Sara, who yipped her disapproval.

Faith watched as Seth found the planter and pulled it out more from the corner it had been in.

"What is so important about that planter? It's just a planter." Faith was bewildered, not sure what was going on any more.

Chapter 11

$\mathscr{P}$aul and Eva stopped on the path, staring at the younger couple, before exchanging glances with one another. Paul shrugged, not quite sure what they were up to.

"Faith? What are you doing? I thought you were to be off your feet."

Her mother's voice had Faith spinning and almost falling until Seth's arm around her stopped her forward motion.

"Mom! You're here! Oh, I am so glad!" She hugged her mother, holding on a bit longer than she normally would, before standing back, her hands in her mother's as she studied the older woman. "Oh, you look wonderful. The pain must be so much better."

"It is, love." She hugged her daughter again, before looking behind her. "And this is Seth. It's been a while. Thank you for all you've done."

He shrugged, feeling that he hadn't really done that much. He moved to walk away, but Paul's hand on his shoulder stopped him.

"I think we'll have to have a talk soon, Seth, but first, what has been going on here? Faith, you're filthy and so is Seth. You look like you've been playing in the woods out back." Amusement lit Paul's face

Seth and Faith looked at themselves and then at one another, breaking out into laughter.

"In a way, we were, Paul." Seth brought them up to date on what had transpired, watching as Paul helped Eva to a seat. Faith had meanwhile bent over the planter, Sara plopping down on her feet.

"Seth. Here. What's in the corner of the planter? I know it's empty of dirt but there's something down there."

Seth reached down, struggling a little to release another tin box. "What is it with your Grandmother and these boxes? How many did she have?"

"A lot, Seth." Eva laughed at her memories. "She loved them, even as a child, she said. She collected them." A look of almost horror crossed her face before she began to laugh almost hysterically, causing the other three to stare at her, not quite sure if she was sane or not. She finally calmed herself down enough to be able to speak, wiping tears from her face. "I just hope she didn't hide them all. I think at last count she had a hundred."

"A hundred?" Seth's voice rose to almost a squeak. "I hope not. That would take forever to find. Do we know where she kept them, so we can count them and figure out how many she hid?"

That question sent both Paul and Eva into spasms of laughter, with Faith suddenly joining in. Seth studied the three, not quite sure what had caused the outburst of mirth.

Faith finally took pity on him. "I don't think we'll have a hundred to find. Something tells me that. And I did find a box of these, but there were certainly more than a hundred in the box. I think she found more, Mom, than what she told you."

Eva laughed heartily again. "Then, we have no idea how many she's hidden. And I would like to know how she managed that feat."

"So would I. Don't open that box yet, kids. Let me go get us some food and something to drink and then we can all look at it." He turned for the door, Seth at his heels, always ready to help.

Eva watched her daughter, not letting her see her glance. Faith had watched Seth walk away, a softening to her features that Eva had not seen before. There had always been something rigid in Faith, ever since she was a child, something that kept people at arm's length, other than a couple of close friends and her parents. That had grieved Eva over the years and driven her to her knees on more than one occasion.

Faith handed her mother the photo they had found, sitting on the floor at her feet, Sara climbing up and settling down on her knee, her muzzle on one wrist, her bright brown eyes watching Eva intently. This was a stranger, she seemed to be saying, and needed to be watched carefully.

"This is when you were two, Faith. You and I had come down for a week. Your father had had to travel for a conference and didn't want us staying on our own. You had such fun that week." Sadness then coloured her face. "It was a couple of years later that for some reason you just refused to come here. We think we know why but we've never been able to talk to you about it. You just refuse, saying you don't know."

"I'm starting to get glimpses of something, Mom, and it scares me, whatever it is. You're right, it's around when I think I was about four or five? I feel so bad. I never knew Grandmother."

"Oh, but you did, love. You did. You loved her dearly and she adored you."

"But how? I don't remember seeing her or talking to her at all."

"That's because she never came as your grandmother." Eva looked up briefly as Paul's hand touched her shoulder and then he set her meal beside her. She watched as Seth handed Faith a plate and then settled himself beside her on the floor, his shoulder lightly touching hers, his hand going out to stroke Sara's head.

"She didn't? Then how?" Faith was puzzled.

"Let's pray and then eat, Faith. We need to talk. This is a talk we've needed to have for years, but your Grandmother refused to let us tell you. She wanted to spend time with you, without memories intruding she said. Once she was in heaven, she said, then we'd talk." Paul prayed for his daughter, knowing that what they had to say would turn her world somewhat upside down and he was afraid, afraid of her shutting down once more, just as she had when a child, or walking away from them.

Faith finally set her plate aside, her hand reaching to bury her fingers in Sara's growing white ruff. Sara sighed contentedly and snuggled closer to Faith, her eyes briefly opening and then closing, knowing all her people, or the people she considered most important, were with her. Seth had watched the emotions flickering across Faith's face as they talked over the meal. He moved his arm so that she could lean against it. She gave him a brief look of thanks before turning to her parents.

"So, we're done our meal. Now, talk, you two. Tell me what it is that you need to." She eyed her parents as they shared a look and her mother's hand went out to her father.

He sighed, breathing a silent word of prayer for guidance and peace, for his daughter as her world would be shaken. He watched Seth, realizing the younger man had eyes only for Faith. Lord, this is in Your hands. We need You to go before us. Please, dear Lord, don't let her be hurt any more than she was, all those years ago, the hurt that she doesn't remember and that Mom Gordon never talked about.

"Dad? Mom?" Faith's voice held apprehension, fear, and resignation.

"Faith, Mom Gordon loved you so much that she was willing to come and see you, using another name to do so." Paul watched his daughter closely. "Whatever happened to you all those years ago, and something did, it affected how you thought of her as Grandmother Gordon. She would never say what it was. I'm still not convinced she knew totally what had happened. You just shut down. You wouldn't talk for a couple of weeks. We had you to our doctor. He could find not a mark on you, nothing that had harmed you in any way, shape or form. But whatever it was, it shut you down. Whenever we would talk about coming here, you would go into hysterics and become sick. Mom Gordon finally said not to force you to come here, that she would come and see you."

"And she did? But I don't understand." Faith looked between her parents before turning her head and looking up at Seth. "Seth, do you know anything?"

He shook his head. "I can vaguely remember Mom and Dad saying you never came any more but I was a kid, anxious to go my own way. I used to come and visit your

Grandmother. She was always so kind to me."

Eva nodded. "That she was, Seth. She adored you, said you were the grandson she didn't have." She sighed, not quite sure how to continue, her hand reaching once more for Paul's. "She said she'd leave a letter for you, but I'm sure that she did." She saw Faith nodding. "You haven't read it yet, then, have you, dear? When you're ready, you will.

"Now, Mom would come and visit. You remember Mrs. Lewis? That was your Grandmother. She would wear a wig and change her makeup and glasses. I think she had a riot as you kids say dressing up and pretending to be someone different."

Paul laughed. "I know she did. She told me that one time. She was there for all your important events, Faith. You adored her, thinking of her as a favourite aunt. When you were young, you would beg for her to come and visit, you wanted to see her so badly. You never asked how she was related to us, or if she was just a friend. You just accepted her and love her."

Faith sank back against Seth's shoulder as his arms came around her. "That was Grandmother? Oh my! I never guessed. She was so much fun. Yes, I loved her. I missed her the last year when you said she was sick and couldn't come. I saved her letters to me." She looked up at Seth. "That's why the handwriting on that letter is so familiar. I've seen it all my life and never knew." Tears flooded her eyes. "Mom, Dad. What did I do?"

Paul was across the floor, kneeling beside her, his arms wrapping around his daughter as Seth moved back, scooping up Sara and cradling her to his chest before he stood and walked off the porch, walking around to the back of the house and sinking down on the chairs near the garden, watching as Sara ran around him.

Chapter 12

The next day, Faith stared at the tin box sitting in front of her on the table. She had been up early, unable to sleep, and had spent hours on her work. Now, tired and grumpy, she sat, listening to her parents talking in the front room before her mother's steps headed her way. Faith reached for the box, sweeping it from the table, and into her pocket, standing as Sara nudged at her leg.

Eva watched her walk away and grieved for the loss of what, she wasn't quite sure. Paul's arms around her comforted somewhat, but she knew there was still a lot ahead of her daughter that she needed to work through. She shivered suddenly, Paul's eyes questioning, but she just shook her head. She could feel danger around her daughter and didn't know who, and that frightened her.

Seth walked towards her just as dusk was falling. She had spent most of the rest of the day, near the garden. Her parents had been in and out, checking on her she knew, but she had needed time to think and pray.

She was desperate to remember what it was that she couldn't, whatever it was that had frightened her so much, and she knew that for a fact, she had been so scared. She could still feel the terror and wanted to know why so that she could move on.

His hand on her shoulder, he paused for a moment, sensing her looking up at him before he glanced down, a smile on his face. She could see the fresh burn on his face and arms.

"You've been outside today, haven't you?" She accused. "Seth, look at that burn."

"It's okay, love. It's okay. It will be tan by morning. That's what happens." He dropped to the grass beside her chair. "And how was your day?"

She shrugged, her eyes on his face as he stared across to the garden. "I managed to get caught up on my work. A few good hours did that for me. I'm just wanting for more to come through. I spent most of the day right here, trying to think through what Mom and Dad said, and trying to remember what happened."

"It will come. Something will trigger it." He poked a finger at the box on the arm of the chair. "You haven't opened it yet."

"No. I was waiting for you, I think. And I'm almost afraid to open it. After the last one."

He reached for it, turning it over and over. "How many do you think she hid?"

Faith shrugged, a smile coming on her face. "I have no idea, but I'm sure she had fun doing it, knowing I'd be searching until I found them all. I never knew it was her, you know? I love that lady so much and never wanted her to leave. I wish they had told me."

"If they had, you might not have loved her or wanted anything to do with her." Seth reached up and stilled the hand she was running along the chair arm. "We'll figure it out, love, between us. We'll get you the peace and answers you need."

She nodded, then tilted her head. "Can I ask you something, Seth?"

"Sure." He waited, finally looked up at her. "What is it?"

"You're always calling me "love". I don't get the impression that's what you call females in your life."

He smiled. "No, I don't. You're special. That's why I call you that." He looked down, somewhat embarrassed at being caught out. He held up the box. "Are you game to open this?"

She huffed, then sighed. "Go ahead. Change the subject."

Seth looked up, seriousness in his eyes. "This is a conversation I would like to revisit at some time, Faith. Right now, it's not the time. Not until we figure out what your Grandmother was up to. I think it's all part of helping you remember what happened."

"I think you're right, and that scares me, Seth. Do I really want to know?"

He nodded. "I think deep inside you do. You have for years."

She sighed again. "You're likely right. Now, mister, open that box."

He grinned as he wiped away the dirt and then worked the lid off. "Well. Well. Well. What do we have here?"

Faith leaned over his shoulder to stare at the object. "A thimble? What is she thinking? I don't sew."

"No, but your Grandmother did. I think I know where to find the next clue." He stood, reaching out a hand for her to take.

She stood, then tugged at her hand, looking up as he refused to let go. "Seth. My hand. Please?"

He shook his head, grinning. "No, can't have my fellow sleuth disappearing and solving the mystery on her own."

Laughing they headed for the house, Sara running excitedly around them before bounding up to bark at the door.

Eva looked around from the stove as they ran through the door. "Faith. Just who I needed to see. Do you remember the dress you had as a youngster. The yellow one? I think that's the one you were wearing in the picture. Something tells me there is more material like that around. If it's still in good condition, I would like to make an apron or two."

Faith shared a look with Seth and nodded. "We're heading up to the sewing room, Mom. I'll look for it." She held up the thimble. "This was the next clue."

"Mom's thimble? I was looking for that today. Now, I know why I couldn't find it." Eva watched as the two headed for the stairs, stopping Sara with a quiet word.

Seth stopped in the doorway, not willing to enter the room. Faith headed in, her eyes searching the room.

"Come on in, Seth. This will take both of us." She sighed. "I need to clear this room. I know Grandmother spent a lot of time here, but I don't sew. Do you know of anyone who could use the materials and everything else?"

"I'm sure Mom would. Just don't give it away. Charge a minimal amount. People today seem to think free stuff is worthless." He poked at a pile of material. "She never got to use this, by the looks of it." He stared around. "Now, where would she have hidden a box in here?"

"Right here." Faith had gone for the sewing basket, lifting the lid and then the tray. "Right in plain sight." She sank into the chair near the sewing basket. "Was she getting tired and too sick, do you think, Seth?"

He shook his head. "No. This is how she used to work the scavenger hunts for us. Some hard, some easy. She said that made it fair for everyone." He sank to the floor at her feet and reached for the box. "Do you want to open it now or after your dinner? Your Mom had it almost ready."

When she didn't respond, he rose, heading for the door. "I'll set this on the table downstairs for you, love."

"Seth?"

He paused, not looking back, his eyes on the box, waiting he thought for her to tell him to leave, that she'd finish the hunt on her own.

"Thank you for everything. You have become a wonderful friend. I don't make friends easily, never have. You just walked right through the barriers around my heart and right into it." Tears sparkled on her lashes as she watched him, knowing that if he ever walked away from her for good, she would be the loser in that.

He finally nodded, moving quietly away, leaving her sitting where she was, lost in her thoughts. She finally rose, hunting for the material her mother had asked her about.

Her hand froze as she reached for it, an image flashing through her mind. An image that drove her to her knees, her mouth open in a silent scream, her eyes shut as tight as she could make them, her hands over her head in a protective manner. She had no idea how long she was there until she finally heard her father's voice, felt his hand lifting her to her feet and then into his arms, carrying her to her own room and gently laying her on the bed.

Paul stepped back as Eva moved to her daughter's side to sit on the edge of the bed, her hand brushing against her hair, then resting on her cheek. Worry etched both their faces. Seth had said she was fine when he left her, that she had planned to look for that material. He had set the box on the kitchen table, letting Eva know where they had found it.

"Faith, dear. What happened?"

Faith shook, her body trembling before she finally calmed enough she could speak. "I found the material, Mom. As I touched it, I saw a horrible image. I didn't get more than a glimpse, but I think someone was killed here on the property. I think I saw it. That's why I wouldn't come back."

Paul bit back the exclamation on his lips, pressing them into a thin line. Eva sat, her hand frozen on her daughter's arm, before she leaned over and just hugged her daughter, her own tears mingling with her daughter's. Paul was on his knees in an instant, his arms around his ladies, his voice raised in prayer and supplication, knowing it would be God that got them through this.

Seth stepped back from his father's front door, asking Paul to step in. As soon as he felt he could leave his ladies, Paul had headed here. Joseph stood in the living room doorway, the newspaper he had been reading in his hands. Seth and his father shared a glance, concern for Paul in their eyes.

"Paul. Come in. Have a seat." Joseph motioned to the couch. "Can I get you anything?" He watched closely as Paul didn't respond, just sat there.

Concern coloured Seth's face as he sat beside Paul. "Is Faith all right? She was when I left her."

Paul shook his head, unable to speak for a moment. When he did, Seth hardly recognized the broken, sorrowful voice.

"She's getting there, Seth. She had a vision when she found that material her mother asked her to look for. That was after you left." He paused, wiping at his eyes, not sure how to continue. The devastation in his eyes when he looked up startled the two other men. "She says she saw someone murdered on her Grandmother's property all those years ago."

"What!" Joseph leaned forward. "She said that?"

Paul nodded, his eyes on Joseph, seeing something there. "What do you know, Joseph? Please. Tell me. I need to help my daughter, and right now I have no idea how to do that."

Joseph shook his head. "How many years ago now was that? Twenty or so?" When Paul nodded, Joseph sat back in his chair, his hand rubbing at his chin. "I can vaguely remember rumours around that time. That someone had disappeared and they didn't know what exactly happened to him. Is that what Faith saw?"

Paul nodded, his eyes still on Joseph. "It could be. I'm not sure, though. She said it was just a glimpse she saw tonight, not enough to know what it was all about."

Seth stared at the two men, then rose, heading for his laptop, returning to sit on the couch again, his internet program open to a search engine. "Okay, year and month, if possible. I can search for any newspaper articles. And then broaden the search if we need to." He paused. "I have a friend who is a private investigator. He can look into it for us, if you choose that route."

"Thank you, Seth. For now, do your research." Paul gave the year and month. "We've always known something had happened, but she wouldn't talk about it. Mom Gordon could never get her to open up. Whatever it was, it happened on the day she was coming home. Early morning, I think, it was. She just shut down. None of us could get her to talk. We were running late, our plane back from the UK delayed for a number of hours. She was actually to have come home the night before." Pain etched his face and eyes. "If she had, this would never have happened, would it? She would have been happy to come and go from her Grandmother and Mom Gordon would not have had to resort to playing another role in order to be in her life."

Seth listened to his father and Paul discuss what had happened, speculate as to who and why. His heart hurt for his friend, knowing that now the images and memories had started, she would have to work it through and she would be in danger if anyone ever thought she was remembering.

He finally looked up. "Dad. Gray Walton? What happened to him? I heard his name the other day and haven't thought of him in years. No one seems to know where he is."

Joseph froze, his hand reaching for his mug, his eyes on Paul, and then turning to Seth. "That's who missing. He hasn't been around in twenty years. No one seems to know where he is or what he's up to. His mother died, not knowing where he was. He didn't come for her funeral five years ago." He sat back, his eyes on his son. "What have you found out?"

"Just that there was an article from around that time, a month or so before, where it was noted that he had been arrested for theft. It was in this area."

"I don't like that, Seth." Paul finally spoke. "Was anyone else involved?"

"The article seems to indicate there was, but he never gave up whoever it was." Seth scrolled through more articles. "It seems that he never showed up for his court date and the authorities could not find him to determine why he hadn't."

"If that's him, then where is he buried?" Paul stared at him, horror coming over him. "You know, it's about that time that Mom Gordon put in that big flower garden. She had a couple of younger men come work it up for her."

Seth sat back, his eyes on the two older men, wondering what the next step would be.

Joseph had looked down, his attention for the moment on the mug he was twisting in his hands. "There is one way to find out if there is a body there." He looked up at Seth, seeing understanding in his son's eyes. "Doesn't Frank have a cadaver dog he's training?"

"He does, Dad. He says he's almost ready to go to his new home. I could ask him if he'd like to check out the area, just as a favour, keeping it quiet what he was doing."

"I would need to talk to the authorities, I think." Paul sat back, his eyes troubled.

"Not yet. We have no evidence that anything is there. Let Frank run his dog and if he hits on anything, then we bring in the police." Seth didn't want Faith disturbed any more than she was. "I'll plan on taking Faith away for the day Frank comes in. She doesn't need to be there."

Paul finally stood to leave, Joseph insisting that they spend time in prayer. Paul had listened to his new friend pray, beseeching God on their behalf, reminding each of them that Christ had prayed for them the Garden all those years ago, that He knew what they would face.

"Would Saturday work? I have to be on job sites for the next couple of days. That I can't get out of." Seth followed Paul out of the door, shutting it behind them.

"It will. She's opened that other box by the way."

"What was in this one?"

Paul shook his head. "A needle. Just a plain needle. She can't figure that one out." Paul looked up as Seth laughed.

"Oh, I get it. A needle in a haystack."

Paul stared at him, then he too laughed. "We never got that connection, Seth, despite all the speculations we came up with. You must have known Mom Gordon well."

"I did. She was a wonderful woman and a wonderful friend. I'll call with the details for Saturday."

Seth watched him drive away, mixed emotions running through him. He wanted to spend the day with Faith, but not like this. Not while a friend searched for a skeleton. He prayed it would not be in her garden. That garden would disappear if that was the case. She would leave and not come back, of that he was certain.

Joseph stood at the front window, his eyes on his son, his heart raised in prayer for the two young people. Now what, Lord? What are Your plans for these two? I know You have a plan for them, and I do pray it's for them to be together. They have fallen in

love with each other over the past few days
and aren't ready or aren't willing to tell each
other. Only in Your timing, dear Lord.

$\mathcal{F}$aith watched as Seth drove away from her home on the Saturday morning. He had appeared the night before, dusty, muddy, tired, sunburnt with the absurd suggestion that she spend the day with him, away from the house. He had a town he wanted to show her, that wasn't the little town of Merritt where she now lived.

"Where did you say we're heading?" She watched the road he had turned on to before accelerating.

"To Oak Landing. It's a small town about thirty minutes from here. Lots of little shops and neat little cafes and restaurants. I thought it might be fun to do something different today. I'm looking for inspiration for a new garden I'm designing. They like antiques and have asked if I can find any old garden statues or stones, or whatever would work."

"Garden statues, huh? We just can't get away from that." She turned to watch him. "Dad told me your suggestion for the needle."

"And?"

"I think you're right. There's an old barn near the back of the property. I was in in briefly. There's straw in there. Do we have to search through that?"

Seth began to laugh, bringing her eyes back to him before she reluctantly laughed with him. "Only if we have to. Somehow, I don't think we will."

"I pray not. I'm not too keen on searching straw by straw." That comment sent him into new spasms of laughter.

She laughed with him as she realized what she had said. "That's not quite what I meant, now is it?"

Hours later, tired, happy and content, Faith settled back into the truck seat, her hand tight in Seth's as he started up the truck and then headed for home. She had objected at first, his holding of her hand, but when he said he didn't want to lose her, she had stopped protesting, realizing how much she liked to have him hold her hand.

Lord, I'm in a lot of trouble right now. Seth is becoming so important to me, but I'm not sure of anything. Not any more. My world has been turned topsy turvy as the lady I now know as my Grandmother would say. You'll have to guide me here, please, dear Lord.

Seth watched the road intently, an uneasy feeling within him. He had felt eyes on them on and off all day but had not seen anyone he could put a finger on. He had watched as Faith had relaxed over the day, finally laughing freely with him and commenting openly about what they were looking at. He had fallen more and more for her as the day went by and was afraid that she would just pack up and leave, if what they suspected was true.

He watched as the lights behind him approached at a rapid pace, ready to pull off to let the vehicle pass, before it roared past him.

"What was that?" Faith turned to watch the truck speed by them.

"Just a crazy driving too fast, I hope." He didn't tell her of his fears, that the truck would be waiting somewhere down the roads and they'd come out the worst of it if it was.

Seth walked Faith to her door, not wanting the day to end, but anxious to here from his father what they had found. He had had a short text about an hour ago, telling him they'd talk when he got home. He looked down at Faith, realizing that she had become so important to him, but afraid to speak.

"Can I give you a lift to church in the morning, Faith, or will you ride with your parents?"

She hesitated, before giving him a shy look. "You can, if you don't mind. Mom and Dad said something about leaving earlier than I usually do. They want to stop at the cemetery on the way."

"Then I will gladly be your chauffeur in the morning. Around 10 work for you?"

"It does." She reached up to drop a kiss on his cheek. "Thank you for today, Seth. I needed that. I have no idea what was going on here, but I had the feeling something was. Let me know what it was when you can."

He watched as the door closed softly behind her before he headed for his truck, his thoughts troubled. How had she known, Lord? We took pains to keep it from her.

Joseph looked up from papers he had spread over the dining room table as Seth walked in, stopping beside his father.

"Dad?" When Joseph didn't speak, Seth dropped into a chair. "You found something."

Joseph sighed, sitting back. "How was your day, son?"

"It was wonderful, Dad. She's such a fun person when she loses track of what brings her down." He groaned. "Did that even make sense? I don't think I am any more."

Joseph smiled, then laughed. "I would say you're in love with a beautiful young lady, Seth. Guard her heart and yours. She's not ready for anything like this yet."

"I know, Dad. That worries me. I'm afraid she'll just pack up and go back to town, and leave me here."

"I don't see that happening. Paul and I talked today. He says she has become more content here that he has seen her ever be. He thinks you're part of it."

Seth shook his head. "If I am, she's hiding it well."

Joseph snorted. "Then you haven't seen how she looks at you. Watch her heart, son. That's all we ask." He poked at the papers on the table, a troubled look coming over his face.

"What did Frank find today?" He could tell something had been found, just by his father's look.

"He found something, but not in her garden. On the other side of the creek, into the town forest. His dog alerted to something. We've talked to the police. They'll bring in a team next week and see what they find. After all this time, it would only be a skeleton, so it might be hard to prove who it is."

Seth sat back, relief in his heart that it hadn't been in Faith's garden. "Then if it's there, what happened? Was it on her property or in the town forest what she saw?"

"It could well have been near the creek. Eva said Faith liked to play along the creek bank, escaping early each morning to go there. She liked to watch the fish and frogs, she would tell them. If she was there and it happened near the property line, she would have had a direct line of sight to them and they to her."

"I'm not liking this, Dad. Not at all. We have no way of knowing who or why, do we?"

"No, we don't. I talked to Reg today. He stopped by when we were out there. I had spoken to him the other day, just to give him a head's up as to what was happening. He seemed to think you were on the right track."

"I hate this, Dad." Seth rose and began to pace, his hand running through his hair and then rubbing at his cheek, stopping as he reached the spot Faith had dropped the kiss earlier. His thoughts momentarily side tracked, he didn't see his father's speculative look.

"What was that, son?" Joseph's voice brought him back to the present.

"I said, I hate this. I was so glad to see her, and now this. When will it end?"

"When you find the last of the boxes, perhaps?" Joseph laughed at the look he was given and held up his hands. "We can do nothing about what Frank found. There may be nothing there, and if there, it will take months perhaps to determine who it is. Meanwhile, you two have a needle in a haystack to track down. Planning on doing that after church tomorrow?"

"We might. What are you and Mom doing after church?" The three usually went out for a meal, giving Martha a break.

"We're planning on taking Paul and Eva out. Are you and Faith joining us?"

Seth shook his head, even as he walked for the door, ready to head for the house he rented. "I'm not sure. I'll ask her tomorrow."

It slipped by him that his father had figured out Seth was planning on taking Faith to church in the morning.

You have it bad, my son. I remember those days. And I can tell already that there will be a number of young ladies jealous of Faith in the morning. You have never escorted any young lady to church before.

Chapter 14

$\mathcal{T}$urning from the sandwiches she was cutting, Faith watched as Seth reached for Sara, cuddling her into his arms, a laugh coming readily from him as she reached to lick at his face, the tongue going even quicker as he protested that he didn't need puppy kisses.

She turned back to the sandwiches, her hand stilling for a moment as she went back to the moment Seth had led her into his church, her hand tight in his. She saw the glances she was given, the speculative looks, the questions on the faces, and on a couple, dislike. Seth, what did you go and do this morning? I get the impression that you don't date, that you've never taken any lady to church, and here you walk in with me, holding my hand, making sure I'm comfortable and taken care of. I guess you've never seen the looks the other ladies have thrown at you.

Seth's hand came down on hers, directing the knife to cut the sandwiches. "They won't cut themselves."

He laughed and moved away from the elbow she threw at him, reaching instead for plates and then into the fridge for the lemonade Eva had prepared that morning.

He seated Faith and then, seating himself beside her, reached for her hand, bowing his head as he led them in prayer.

Their meal finished, Faith headed for her garden, Sara in her arms, her face down against her soft black coat. She grown to love this puppy, but what was she do to, when, if, she went back to town? Having lived in the house here, she was no longer adamant that she had to be in town. There was a peace she found here she had not found elsewhere, even though she was troubled by being here.

Seth's arm came around her shoulder in silent comfort. She leaned against him, knowing he was asking for nothing but friendship from her, even if that was all she had to give. Lord, I'm falling in love with him, but I don't know how he feels. And I don't know if I plan to stay here. Oh, this is so frustrating, Lord. I have no idea what to do. That's so unlike me.

Seth turned her towards the buildings. "I've been thinking about that needle. The common saying to find a needle in a haystack. Your Grandmother doesn't have hay any longer. She didn't buy any last fall, but she still has straw. Think that would work?"

Faith stared at the buildings, bending over to let Sara run loose. "It might." She walked that way, Seth's hand catching hers. She was liking this a lot, she thought. More than I should, but she didn't try and take her hand back. She had lost that battle with her heart yesterday. "Which building? I must confess I've been avoiding them."

"The third one. It's not real large, for a barn, but it was enough to keep the pony in."

"Pony?" Faith looked up at him as he slid the door to the barn open. "She had a pony? I didn't know that."

"She did." Seth sighed, knowing it was once more up to him to explain something about her Grandmother. "The pony would have been close to thirty years old. She bought it when you were a toddler, just for you. She didn't have the heart to get rid of him, you loved him so much. Even when you didn't come back, she held on to the memories. He became very ill last fall and with his age, they decided he needed to be given a rest. He's buried down near the creek, near where you used to like to play."

Sorrow covered her face. "I never knew. There's so much I never knew." Her voice was barely above a whisper

Seth's heart broke for her, and his hand came up, the back of his fingers stroking down her cheek, catching the tears that had fallen. "She understood, my love. She understood, much more that you'll ever know, here on earth at least."

He looked around. "Now, where would the next box be?"

"That's a good question. Where would she put it?" Faith moved towards the shelves on the wall, searching them, and then moving towards a cupboard, coming away empty from it. She looked around, not seeing Seth for a moment.

"Seth? Where are you?" She turned as she heard a noise, then voices outside. She spun, hitting Seth as she did so.

"Seth? There's someone out there!" Her voice was barely above a whisper.

"I know. Come on. There are some bales of straw back here. We can slip down behind them. For some reason, they are piled with an opening behind them." He helped her over the bales, dropping down beside her, his arms coming around her. They barely breathed, hearing the two men.

The men searched the barn, their voices getting louder, the words more foul as they came up empty.

"I heard them say it was in here. But it's not. Where is it?" The gruffer voice was angry, Faith could tell, not wanting them to find them, knowing instinctively it would not go well.

Seth's arms tightened around her, and she hid her face against him. She could feel the accelerated beating of his heart, the shallow breaths he was taking. They waited until they heard the men move away, the door banging open and shut idly after them.

Faith finally sat back. "They're gone?"

"I think so. Wait here. I'll go check."

Her hand caught his as he went to stand. "Please be careful. If they see you, they'll come back for me."

"I know, my love. Trust me. They won't see me." He was gone, up and over the bales of straw before she could say a word.

Her heart beating hard, she prayed for safety, for Seth, for herself. She moved her hand in the straw, hearing a faint click. She paused, her eyes looking up, then back down as she carefully worked to move the straw, trying her best not to make a sound.

Seth peered over the bales, leaning on a hand as he watched her. He knew she wasn't aware he had come back, and that worried him.

"Faith?"

"Yes, Seth. I know you're there. I heard something click here in the straw. I'm trying to find it." She raised her hand, a triumphant look on her face. "And I did. Another box."

She handed it to him as she stood, watching as he tucked it into a pocket, and then took the hands he extended to her, standing in the circle of his arms once she was over the bales. She moved away, walking to the door, hesitating as she looked back.

Seth stood watching her before he looked down, shaking his head. He had been so worried about her and she seemed so unconcern. That was, until he came closer and saw the fear still in her eyes.

"Let's head for the house. Sara is already at the door, I saw when I was looking around."

Her parents were in the living room when they ran through the back door, breathless. They looked up at the younger couple before exchanging glances.

"We found another box." Faith shot a look at Seth, daring him to say anything else

He shook his head and decided he had been doing that a lot since Faith arrived. "That we did. In the barn, behind a carefully piled stack of straw bales. There is no way your Grandmother did that."

"No, of course not. I think she's had help and that someone is from around here." Faith studied Seth, deciding it wasn't him. He was to surprised at their finds. "Who would help her?"

"It could be anyone, my love. She could have hired a student, letting them think it was a hunt for a youth group."

"But wouldn't they wonder why it never happened?"

"Not if it was just before she passed away. That would explain why it didn't happen."

She nodded, her eyes on him, narrowing at she watched his eyes flick between her and her father. She shook a finger at him, not letting her parents see her. "Now, let's open this box. I have no idea where she'd send us next. How many buildings are left?"

"Three, I think, if you count the chicken coop. It's so tiny, though." Seth laughed at the face she made at him, handing her the box.

She sat, her hands on it, not moving. She seemed lost in thought. Her mother's hand on her arm brought her back to the present.

"I remember these boxes, Mom. Grandmother let me play with them. All we've found so far. Let me think." She stared into the distance, not seeing the surprise on her companions' faces.

"You played with these boxes, dear?" Eva's voice brought her back to the room.

"I did, Mom. I can remember that. Grandmother would put treats in them and I would work to open them. She had so many, but there were only certain ones I wanted to play with. They all had dogs or puppies on them." She raised her eyes. "Is she the one, Seth?"

He shrugged from where he had taken a seat on the floor near her. "She could be. It would be like her to do just that."

"Just what?" Paul was puzzled, not sure how that comment fit in with the boxes.

Seth reached for Sara, who was sitting watching him. "Sara. She just appeared at the door. I checked with my friend and he said someone had purchased her for Faith."

"You never told me that, Faith. Just that you had a puppy show up at your door."

"Well, she did just that. Whoever bought her wanted to remain anonymous. I've left it at that." She stared down at the box in her hands, somehow knowing this was a game changer. That this one would send them off somewhere, and that somewhere would be into danger. She knew her Grandmother would never do that knowingly, but whoever those men were, they were determined to find the treasure Faith had waiting for her.

Seth reached to still her hands, his strong and firm on hers. "Let's pray about this one, my love. I think it's going to change something in the hunt."

She nodded. "I know, Seth. After what just happened, I'm afraid."

"I know." He didn't see the looks her parents were giving one another before looking at them.

Faith finally opened the box, her hand stilling as she held the lid over the box. A frown appeared.

"Seth?"

He rose, sitting on the couch beside her, his hand reaching for the box. "What is it?"

"That I have no idea. I have never seen anything like this before." She raised her eyes, a frown in place. "Have you?"

He looked in the box, then with gentle fingers, withdrew the object, placing it into his hand and looking at it in better light. "I have, my love. It's a stone, but not from here. I know I've seen it somewhere though."

Paul rose, his eyes on the stone. "It's from the river in town, Seth. There are certain stones there that are smooth and that coloured. Mom Gordon said the kids used to toss them in, making wishes on them."

Eva drew in her breath, remembered pleasure lighting her face, so much like her daughter's. "Oh, I remember that. We had so much fun. We made so many wishes on those stones. Someone provided a pile whenever the stones were getting few in number, but he's gone now. He was an older gentleman when I was young. I know we were so disappointed when he passed on and the stones disappeared. The boys used to dive in and find as many as they could, just so we could continue that." She looked at Faith's stone. "But I don't remember one that translucent green."

"No, I have never seen one that colour." Seth looked down at Faith, her head almost touching his arm as she stared at the stone. "Looks as if we have a trip to town one night, Faith, to see where the next box is."

Chapter 15

$\mathcal{F}$aith watched the next night as Seth wandered the river bank. He had seated her in a park bench, told her to stay right where she was, and he would search for the box. So far, he hadn't had any luck.

"Where would she have put it?" Seth was at a loss. "She didn't walk this far, not in the last few months. Unless her conspirator placed it for her."

"Somehow, I think she did this one. She would have made herself walk this far." She rose, eyes searching, before she wanted towards a sign. "What about here, Seth? Could it be here somewhere?"

"You may be right." He searched around the double-sided sign, finally reaching down inside. "I found it. I can't grab it though."

"Let me try." Faith reached down, her fingers feeling the box before she could finally grasp it. "I have it." She withdrew it, staring at the photo on it. "I do remember this one. She used to put small chocolate candies in it, as a treat for after supper." She blinked back tears. "I feel like I lost so much when I refused to come back."

Seth hugged her before leading her back to the bench. "Sit. Catch your breath and then we'll take a look at the box."

She nodded, her eyes distant with memory. "Mom and Dad tried to hard to get me to come here. I can remember that now. Dad would even detour around, trying to fool me. I would become so upset I would be physically ill. They finally had to stop trying that. I guess that's when they came up with the plan for Grandmother to disguise herself. I always thought that lady was so much fun."

"She was fun, Faith. She would have loved the chance to dress up and pretend to be someone else. Whenever the church would put on a skit or a play, she was always in it. She would bring down the house if it was a comedy." He hugged her again. "I know you're hurting, my love, but she did become part of your life. And you have so many memories just for you."

She nodded. "I still regret that, Seth. But I can't change the past. I just remember I couldn't come here and I'm still not sure why."

She studied the box in front of her, handing it over to him. "It's your turn, I think."

"We're taking turns now, are we?" He smirked as she stared at him, not quite sure if he was serious or not.

"I guess we are." She smiled. "Now, open it, please."

"You sound like a little kid at Christmas, hardly able to wait for your gifts."

"That would be about right. I was always up really early, sitting on the stairs, staring into the dark living room, excited as everything but knowing I couldn't go in there until Mom and Dad were up."

"I was the same, only I had to stay in bed until Mom or Dad came and got me. That was torture." Seth laughed at the memories, knowing that they were part of who had made him the man he was.

He worked at the box, finally lifting the lid, staring down into the box, then at her.

"This is getting more bizarre, Faith. I have no idea where we're heading next. I would say back to your place and one of the other buildings."

She looked down into it. "A square nail. They're really old, aren't they?"

"That they are. I know the fourth building was built with them." He closed the lid and just sat, thinking about everything they had found so far. "I have no idea what the idea is behind these, do you?"

She shook her head. "I have no idea." She turned, feeling watched again. "I haven't read her letter as yet. I keep putting it off. I'm not sure if I will."

"You need to. At some point. It may explain what this is all about."

"In that case, maybe I should read it now."

Seth laughed as he pulled her to her feet, walking hand in hand with her back to the truck. "Somehow, I think she knows you would put off reading it until the very end. That's the kind of understanding she had."

"I am coming to see that." She paused as he helped her into his truck, her hand on the seatbelt. "Seth, why do I feel like danger is closing in on us?"

"I know. I can feel it too. Something tells me we're far from finished with those men. They seem to think you have this huge treasure you're looking for and that it's worth a fortune. It may be worth something in money, but knowing your Grandmother, it is something that has an unearthly, heavenly wealth to it."

"That's what I'm thinking." She sighed as she watched him drive away from town. "But I just don't know how it will end and that scares me."

"I know it does. It scares me too. I definitely do not want to see you or your parents hurt in any way."

She. nodded. "I know. I don't either. Dad said today they'll be here until Thursday, then they have to head back that afternoon. Mom has appointments on Friday, and he has to check in with his work. I think he's planning on retiring soon, just from what he said today."

"Is that right? Why do you say that?"

She shrugged. "Just he said he won't be working there much longer and he wanted to make sure that his replacement was up to speed on what he needed to know. Dad has always wanted to retire early, to travel on short term missions, and work in some of the missions in the down town area of our town. He has a heart for those men who are down and out."

"That's a wonderful plan for retirement." Seth paused, not quite sure how to ask the next question.

"No, Seth. I'm not leaving with them. I've talked it over with them and then with the publisher I work for. My home is here now. I feel like I am where I should be, finally."

"You are? That's great." He didn't know what to say, feeling suddenly tongue tied.

She began to laugh. "As if you were hoping I was leaving soon. I can read you, Seth Logan. You don't want me to leave anymore than I want to leave. Is that bold enough for you?"

He reached for her hand and gripped it tightly for a moment. "It tells me exactly what I wanted to know. Thank you, Miss Webster, for being so bold."

She shook her head at him. "Seth Logan, I do declare, you're blushing." She laughed at his discomfort, then changed the subject.

Seth walked back to his truck after Faith had locked the door after herself. It was late and she was tired, she told him. It had been a long day.

Seth sat for a moment before he headed home. Tomorrow was an early day for him, he needed to be on a job site, but with the way his business was growing, he would soon be able to hire someone who could do that for him, leaving him to work his magic with his plans.

He puzzled out the nail, trying to figure out just what Mrs. Gordon had meant by it. He knew there was a meaning to each of the clues, there always had been when she set up a scavenger hunt. That had been the biggest part of the fun for him, trying to figure out her meanings. He knew eventually he would with these. He prayed fervently that God would keep his lady safe.

Walking up to his front porch, lost in thought, he didn't see the dark form waiting there or the second one coming up behind him. He didn't sense their presence until he was down on the sidewalk, a knee grinding into his back, one arm behind him, the other held to the ground by a booted foot.

"Where is it?"

He recognized the voice from the barn. Shaking his head, he denied knowing what the men wanted, no matter how many times or how he was asked. He fears for Faith, hearing them threaten her.

"She doesn't know either. We haven't found it."

"I say you have. Why would you be running all over like you are? You know what it is."

"No, we don't."

Finally, he convinced them he had no idea what it was or where it was. The knee ground deeper into his back before the man rose, a kick to his ribs sending him back to the ground.

He heard a vehicle drive away before he rose shakily to his feet. He searched for his keys, seeing them off to the side on the grass. Bending to pick them up, he almost fell once more. He sank to his front steps, his hand to his ribs, feeling them. Not broken, he thought, just bruised. He worked to regain his breath, knowing he still had to rise and walk up the steps. He looked over his shoulder. The steps seemed to be huge tonight, he thought, wearily rising and gripping the handrail to guide his steps. A shaky hand inserted the key into the lock before he pushed the door open, closing and locking it behind him.

He sank to his knees, his hands on the floor in front of him. He finally rose, dropping his hat on the table near the door, his keys beside it and headed down the hall to his bedroom, his hand running along the top of the wainscotting to help him balance. He sank face down onto the bed for a moment, before he flopped to his back, groaning with pain as he did so. His eyes closing, he slept, knowing he would be awake early. I'm sorry, Lord. I just can't do my devotions tonight. I'll do double tomorrow. Keep my lady safe, please, God?

He rose early the next morning, spending time in prayer, specific in his requests and pleas for Faith. Somehow, he knew she was in more and more danger each day. He also knew her Grandmother wouldn't have wanted that and if she had known what would have occurred, she would never have set up the scavenger hunt for Faith.

Chapter 16

Faith searched the building the next day, on a hunt for the next box. She had spent a good portion of her day on her work, and welcomed a chance to get outside. Sara romped around her, her tail wagging steadily at the attention she was getting.

Faith sighed, stepping back from the last cupboard. "I don't see anything, Sara. I was sure this was the building. It's the one Seth said had the old nails. It's the oldest one here." She dropped to a wooden box, her hand scratching Sara's ears. "Just where would she have put it?"

Her eyes searched the building once more, turning to follow the line of the walls before she frowned and rose, heading for the corner of the building behind her. She crowed in triumph.

"I have it, Sara. Now, all I need is for Seth to stop by and we can open it." She stuck it into her pocket and then shutting the door tightly, ran for the house, dodging the drops of the rain that had just started.

Her mother looked around. "Here you are, dear. It's almost time for supper. Get yourself washed up, or do you have to feed your dog first?"

"Sara first and then I'll wash up. Has Seth called?"

"No, he hasn't that I know of. He didn't call me, if that's what you're asking. I've heard your phone ringing but I didn't go near it." Her mother smiled at the look Faith threw her before she hugged her.

Faith nodded. "I'll check when I wash up. Come on, Sara, suppertime. Let's get you fed."

Faith picked up her phone, shooting a glance at the door behind her. She knew her parents were in the kitchen and she hoped they stayed there. Seth had called a couple of times today, leaving voice messages for her both times. She regretted that she had been on a conference call when he had left them.

She frowned. No call from him. That was odd. He had been calling regularly lately and she had come to depend on that. She laid her phone back down and then sank to the edge of her bed. What am I to do, Lord? She pulled out the box, her thumb rubbing across the picture, then sighing, rose, dropping it back into her pocket. Maybe Seth would stop by tonight. If not, she'd wait for him before she opened it. This time, the urge to turn and run as fast and as far as she could overcame her and she staggered, her hand going to the wall to brace herself.

She pulled herself together, knowing if she didn't her mother would question her. She would have to wait until later to fall apart.

She sat with her parents after their meal, listening to them talk, but not hearing their words. She finally excused herself, heading for her bedroom. She checked her phone. No, he had not called, and she would not call him. She reached for her Bible, with it falling open to one of her favourite passages, John 17. She read the prayer in the garden and once again paused as she realized that she had been prayed for, by her Saviour himself.

She finally fell asleep on top of the covers, reaching during the night for a light blanket. Her sleep was broken, as she tossed and turned, forgotten memories finding their way into her dreams and scaring her. She awoke in the very early morning hours, scooped up Sara and the tin box, and crept down the stairs. Her phone was in her pocket as were her keys.

She had to go somewhere but where, she wondered? Where could she find the peace she needed this morning? She was scared and her Grandmother's scavenger hunt was almost too much right now. Why, Grandmother, why this? What were you telling me? Do I need to read the letter and find what you wanted me to find? How do I know how many more boxes you've hidden are out there?

She paused as she walked towards her car, a frown on her face. A truck sat behind her car and she recognized it. She walked towards it, tapping at the passenger window and then climbing in, to sit and stare at Seth.

"Seth? What happened last night? Why are you here?"

He scrubbed hands down his face, the sound rough against the stubble on his face. "I'm sorry, Faith. I thought I would get here in time to talk to you, but the lights were out. We had major issues on the job site. I couldn't even get away to call you." He watched as she nodded, relief showing on her face.

"I thought something had happened to you. Something bad." She saw him flinch. "It did. What happened, Seth?"

"I was attacked by those two men Monday night as I walked up to my door. They want whatever it is you're looking for."

"Well, that much we knew. But there's more, isn't there?"

He nodded, pain showing briefly as he moved to take her hand, his thumb running over the back of it, his grip warm and comforting to her. "There is. They're threatening you, Faith, and I don't know how to protect you."

She sighed. "I just knew it. I felt something last night. I had so many memories coming at me, I can't tell what is real and what isn't." She studied him, seeing the fatigue in his face and hearing it in his voice. "What time do you need to be on site?"

"I don't have to today. With the problems yesterday and staying late, we've worked out what we needed and the landscaper is on his own today. He should be fine. I do need to do some work though." He stared out the window, his eyes narrowing as he thought. "What are you up to today?"

"I have a couple of hours work on a manuscript, then I have to make a call to the publisher about the next book." She tugged at his hand. "Come on in. I'll make us some coffee. And if you want, you can have a shower."

"That sounds wonderful, my love." His hand on her arm let her know to stay put until he came around, a smile on his face for her as he helped her from and then walked back to the house with her. "Where were you off to?"

She shrugged. "I have no idea. I just needed to get away." She stopped in her walk, Sara running into the back of her legs and protesting that. She looked up at him, her heart in her eyes. "I think I was looking for you. You make me feel safe and secure, Seth. I needed that. After all the dreams last night." She dug into her pocket and pulled out the tin. "And I found this. I was looking at it last night and felt fear like I have never before felt it."

His hand on her cheek, he watched her face before he bent and kissed her, then hugged her to him. "We'll get there. I don't think you're going to find many more. This may be the last one, but I don't think it is. She has a meaning for each of them. I just haven't figured it out."

She turned in his arms and wrapped one of hers around him, urging him up the stairs. "Have your shower while I make coffee and some breakfast. You didn't eat last night, now did you?"

He laughed softly at the scolding tone in her voice. "No, I didn't. By the time we finished, it was dark and I just didn't feel like eating. I just wanted to come and find you."

"That's where I think I was headed this morning. I needed to talk to you." She reached into her pocket. "I found the box in the building you said it would be in. But when I touch it, I feel such fear, Seth. And I don't know why."

His hands closed over hers and his head dropped to lay on hers. "God is here, my love. No matter what happens, He is here. Trust him on that."

"I do. It's just so hard." She stepped back. "Now, get yourself cleaned up. I'll have your coffee ready when you're out."

He stood for a moment, watching her walk away from him, praying that she never did just that for real. He was thankful she had wanted to run to him, but he knew they weren't through with those men, not by a long shot. He stared down at Sara, who sat, leaning hard against his leg, and then scooper her up to hug her, dodging the tongue that worked rapidly to find his face.

"Faith?"

She turned as she heard her father's voice. "Dad? You're up early."

He reached past her for the coffee and poured their mugs full, seeing an extra and knowing Seth was there. "Seth is here? It's early."

"I know. He spent last night outside in his truck. He got here after we had turned the lights out. Something about a problem on his job site and that he couldn't get away until then."

"He's got it bad, you know." Mischief lurked in his eyes as he tried not to smile as she spun, mouth open to speak before she snapped it closed. "And so do you." Her father hugged her. "Go with it, sweetheart. Seth is a good man and he loves you as much as I think he does, you'll have a wonderful life. Just like your Mom and I."

She nodded against his shoulder, then stepped back. "Thanks, Dad. Now, sit. I have breakfast ready. Mom's not up yet?"

"No, she's still sleeping. I don't think she slept very well last night. She was really restless."

"That makes two of us."

Before Paul could ask what she meant,
she had turned away to greet Seth.

Chapter 17

*T*urning the box idly over and over in his hands, Seth watched Faith as she cleaned up from their meal. Paul had excused himself, something about a call he was expecting.

Faith sat back at the table, her finger poking at the box. "Open it. I can't. Not that one. It makes me too frightened."

Seth reached for her hand and bowed his head, praying for wisdom and protection for them. He knew it would end soon, whatever it was, and he didn't want his lady hurt. Though how he could prevent just that, he wasn't sure. Not when he was blindsided himself the other night.

He studied the lid, seeing the little black and white dog on it. "This looks like Sara." She nodded, her eyes on his, fear lurking in them. "I wonder how many your Grandmother did hide and how she managed to get around to do just that."

"Unless we find her co-conspirator, we likely will never know." She sighed. "It has to be someone from church or from town, someone she trusted deeply and who was willing to help carry out her plans even after she passed on."

Seth nodded. "I've a list of names I came up with but honestly? I have no idea who it would be."

She nodded, reaching for the box and working at the lid. When it loosened, she hesitated, her eyes going to Seth.

"I have the feeling, Seth, that when I take the lid off this one, it will change everything we've been through. So far, it's been fun, in a weird way. This one, I sense it's more serious. I'm not sure I'm ready for that."

"I think you are, my love." He reached to still her hand, his covering hers on the box lid. "We can leave it and stop the hunt. We don't have to finish it. You can read your letter from her and know what she wanted you to find. It's your decision." He paused, biting at his upper lip, his eyes thoughtful as he stared out the large window near the table, seeing the growth in the garden.

She finally moved, shifting his hand from hers, hers fingers tapping on the box lid before she removed it. She had her eyes on him, seeing his love and trust in her before she looked down. A frown came over her face.

"What is this? Seth? What is she doing now?"

He reached for the box, staring down at it. "Now, that's interesting. What was she thinking?" He pulled out the tiny gold cross. "This looks like it is a child's cross."

"It is, Seth. Faith, that was yours. It disappeared when you were tiny, about the time you refused to come back. I wonder if Mom found it and then saved it to give to you, forgetting she had it until now." Eva had stopped behind Seth's chair.

"Mine? I don't remember it at all." Faith looked up at her mother, seeing the fatigue on her face and the dark circles under her eyes. "Sit, Mom. I'll get your tea."

Eva watched as her daughter moved around the room, continuing her conversation with Seth. The younger couple were puzzled, not sure where they were being sent next.

"The church, I would think, Seth. Somewhere on the outside. I'm not familiar enough with it now to know where she would have hidden something."

Seth looked outside, seeing the rain starting again. "We can't search today, not with the rain. Faith, thank you for breakfast. I really do need to run." He reached to kiss her and then walked away. She followed him, their conversation light and teasing.

Paul stood for a moment, watching them, knowing something had changed with them before he headed to find Eva.

"What's going on with those two, Paul?" Eva set her mug back down.

"I think they've discovered they love one another." His voice was low. "Faith said Seth was sitting outside in his truck this morning. He had come to find her last night. Only all the lights were out."

She nodded, as she rubbed her hand on his arm. "It's happening, isn't it, love? Our girl has grown up and found a love of her own."

He sighed. "That she has. And I couldn't be happier. You know me. I just had to lose her."

Eva laughed at that. "You're not losing her, Paul. We're getting the son we could never have."

He laughed at her words. "That we are. Listen, we're still on for tomorrow afternoon? I hate to leave when things are still so unsettled with Faith."

"We are, and we have no choice. I have those appointments on Friday. How did your call go this morning?"

"It's all set. Management has agreed to my proposal. I can retire in two weeks, taking my sick time and vacation time to work out the rest of my notice." He looked around, not seeing Faith. "I have a surprise for Faith too."

Eva's mouth opened to ask what it was, then snapped shut as she heard steps coming back into the kitchen. She and Paul would talk later.

Faith stood, later that day, on the back porch, one arm around a support post, her eyes on the horizon, her thoughts on the Grandmother she had known, without knowing she had. Lord, I have no idea why things are working out the way they are. But You do. You are in control. Let me rest in that. She paused in her prayer, a thought niggling at her mind. She turned, then almost ran for her office, scrabbling through the paperwork she had on her desk, then searching the drawers. She knew she had that paper, had had it for years.

She paused, a hand to her throat, as she thought, finally running for the stairs and her bedroom, searching her purse and then her overnight bag. She sank back on the floor. Yes, she did have it. She stared at the envelope, not sure what to do with it.

How did it fit in, she wondered? She pulled open the envelope, and the unfolded the paper from within it, studying the diagram on it. What does it mean? She would need to show it to Seth. He had promised to stop by in the later afternoon and it was getting close to that time. She headed back down the stairs, knowing that her parents would be leaving on the next day and wanting to spend some time with them.

She didn't want to see them leave but her fear for their safety had increased with each day they were there. She didn't want to see them hurt, and that would happen, she just knew, if they stayed.

Eva watched her daughter from her seat in the living room, a frown covering her face. Now what was it she had found? It was something, she knew, something that she didn't want to tell her about.

Seth stood for a moment, his eyes searching the face of the woman he had come to love deeply, before he moved to envelope her into a hug. She clung to him, and he could feel the shudders running through her.

"Faith? What happened?"

"I found a diagram when I was younger. I think Grandmother left it behind. I brought it with me for some reason. I really have no idea what it is." She stepped back, her eyes looking towards the living room. "It's stopped raining. Can we go look around the church? I need to talk to you about that paper, but I don't want to here, where Mom and Dad can hear us."

They walked the perimeter of the church, searching for the box they knew they would find, not seeing it at all.

"What if it's not the church? We just assumed it would be, given that it's a cross." Faith chewed at her bottom lip, trying hard to think of where the next box would be.

"I still think it's here somewhere. I'm just not sure where." He spun in a circle, his eyes on the cemetery. "I have an idea. Let's search the cemetery.

"Are you kidding me? Search there?" She ran to catch up with him. "Seth? You are serious."

"I am. There's one grave that has a tall cross near it. Maybe that's where the next box is."

She stared at him for a moment, standing where he had once more walked away from her, before she ran after him, catching at his arm. "Seth, please. Stop. Talk to me. You've come up with an idea."

"I have. Do you have that diagram with you?"

She nodded, pulling it out and handing it to him. "It doesn't make sense to me. Just a bunch of numbers and symbols."

Seth wrapped an arm around her, pulling her close to his heart as he unfolded the paper. "Let's see. So far, we're at number nine with the boxes. This diagram has ten numbers on it. Faith." His voice died away as he stared at the paper, dumbfounded at what he was seeing. "This is her plan. She always drew a diagram of what she was doing with the hunts. She must have lost it when she was visiting you."

"It is? Why wouldn't I have known that?"

"Because you never had the chance to work one of her hunts. There are variations from this as to what we've been finding and where, but I think this is the basis for it." He looked up, his eyes narrowing as he searched the area in front of him. "There. There's the cross."

He moved away, Faith standing just where he had, her hands on her mouth, as a sudden vision overcame her. She dropped to her knees, the pain she felt that deep within her.

Seth searched around the cross, seeing the box and pulling it out, turning to speak with Faith. Not seeing her, he tucked the box into a shirt pocket and walked slowly back towards where he had last seen her. His steps halted and then he was running towards her, down on his knees and gathering her close

"Faith? Talk to me. What happened?"

When she didn't answer, just turned her head into his shoulder, he was on his feet, staggering a moment until he got his balance and then almost running for his truck. He tucked her inside and ran around to the driver's side, sliding in, his hand reaching for hers.

"Faith? What happened? Did you get stung by a bee or something?" Worry coloured his words and he felt like he wasn't thinking straight.

She shook her head and with that movement, she wept, finally swiping at her tears, taking the towel he handed her.

"No. It just happened again. I had such a feeling of pain and worry and terror the night I was looking at the last box. I had it again, Seth. We're in trouble and I don't know who from or how it will hit."

He searched her face, seeing the terror still lurking there. Lord, what now? I know we're facing something here that we can't control or won't see coming. Please, dear Lord, protect my lady.

She finally pointed to his shirt pocket. "You found the box. What's in it?"

He pulled it out. "I have no idea, my love. I'm not sure I'm ready to open it, not yet."

"We have to, Seth." She reached for it and then froze, the terror back on her face.

Seth froze, seeing the agony on her face, before he pried the box from her fingers, setting it on the console and then reaching to wrap her in his arms as best he could.

"That's what I was afraid of, Faith. Somehow, you're picking up on something with these last couple of boxes."

She nodded, her eyes on the box. How did she open this one now, feeling as she did?

His hand came down on hers again. "Leave it for tonight, my love."

She finally looked up, seeing the concern on his face. "I will. Can you take me home, please?" Her voice held a wobble he had never heard before.

Lord, please be with my lady. I can't be all the time and I am so afraid for her.

Chapter 18

$\mathscr{F}$aith stood by the creek, her eyes on the flowing water, then raising them to stare across at the trees on the town side of the pasture. Activity was going on there, and she knew why. No one had told her, but she just knew they were digging up the ground. Rumours had reached her that Seth's friend and his dog had found something. She shivered, a sudden chill running down her back. It was Saturday afternoon, and Seth had promised he would be around shortly.

She turned as she heard footsteps behind her. She saw Seth's mother, Martha, approaching.

"Faith, dear. I wondered if you would be here when I didn't get an answer at your door. This is so peaceful. Your Grandmother spent a lot of time here, even with your Grandfather was alive. She called it her thinking corner or her prayer corner, depending on her mood."

Faith nodded. "I thought that. It is peaceful. Except for that." Her eyes raised once more to watch the activity on the horizon.

"Yes, that. Seth said he hadn't had a chance to talk to you yet. We've had word that the investigators did find a skeleton. They're still working to remove it." She reached out an arm, hugging Faith before turning her back to the house. "Come, dear. This will not help you any to stand and watch that. The investigator will be around later today, I think he said."

Faith nodded, a sadness overwhelming her, that she tried to shake off and couldn't quite manage.

"Mrs. Logan, you knew my Grandmother well. Why would she have sent me on a scavenger hunt?"

Martha stood for a moment at the kitchen counter, her hand rubbing along the edge. "That, my dear, I have no idea why. She could be interesting, to say the least. She had plans for you that I don't think she wanted to have to put into place. Part of that was bringing you back her to face what happened when you were young. None of know exactly what that was."

Faith shuddered as she slid into a chair, her arms wrapping around herself. "It has to do with whatever they're digging up back there. Seth knows part of it. I think I saw someone killed when I was young and they threatened me. As long as I stayed away, I was safe. Now that I'm back, they'll come after me. They're also after whatever the treasure is that Grandmother left."

"And if there is no earthly treasure, other than this house, what are your feelings on that?"

"I would fine with that. I don't need a lot. Just what I have. I have work that I enjoy immensely, family, some close friends. A God who does me intensely. What more do I need?" She finally looked up as Martha stayed silent. "Mrs. Logan?"

"Please, call me Martha. I think we're going to be neighbours." Martha had seated herself, her eyes on her young friend, her heart raised in prayer. "I think you need and desire to be loved for just being you, to have the love of someone just your own. Am I correct?"

Faith finally nodded. "I used to think I was unloveable except to my family. Now, I'm not so sure."

Martha reached for her hands, hers work worn and rough, but warm on Faith's. "You are such a loving person, Faith. I can see it even though we have not had a lot of contact. At least, not yet." Faith's eyes never left her face, giving her a reason to continue. "Seth has not spoken much about his feelings. But I can tell you, he has never dated. He has never spent time with a young lady like he has with you. That tells me you're important to him."

Faith nodded. "I think we're both coming to that conclusion. I worry though that he'll get hurt trying to help me. I don't want that."

Martha laughed, her eyes so much like her son's lighting up as she did so. "That, my dear, is something you can't prevent. He has staked his claim on you, taking you to church the way he has. He's not done that before."

"I thought that. I'm not sure what to think. I haven't been able to talk to Mom. She's been too worried about me. And then with her surgery and that, I didn't want to bother her."

"My dear, something like this is never a bother. If I had a daughter, I would have loved for her to come and share with me the feelings she was trying to sort through, to walk with her the journey of a first love and a lasting love, knowing my son." Martha rose, hugging her tightly, and then stepping back. "I think this is why I had such a burden to come and see you today, Faith. If you can't talk to your own mother, come find me." She walked away, the door closing quietly behind her.

Seth stood for a moment, watching the landscaper work his magic at a home in town. It was a big task, bigger than he had envisioned, the home owner wanting to make his place a showcase. So far, Seth knew, he had been well pleased with the design and the work. Another couple of weeks would see this one completed. He frowned, knowing his mind was not totally on his work. Quitting time could not come soon enough, he decided.

Faith stood for a moment, watching Seth, before she spoke to one of the workman, who nodded and headed for Seth. She saw him stop for a moment by Seth, who spun, his eyes searching for her. He spoke to the supervisor for a moment, before he walked towards her, pulling off his hard hat as he did so, and tossing it through his open truck window.

He stopped in front of her, then hugged her tightly. "This is a nice surprise. I like this."

She hugged him back, desperate to feel the safety and security she felt with him. "I just needed to see you."

"That's still nice. I have another hour here, then I'm done." He looked around. "Where's your car?"

"At home. I hitched a ride in with your Dad. I was hoping some tall handsome man might be so kind as to give me a lift home."

"This tall handsome man would be delighted to. Here, come sit in the shade. The owners won't mind. In fact, if they come home, they'll take you into the house. They were good friends of your Grandmother's."

She sighed. "It sounds as if everyone was." She bit her lip. "I apologize. That didn't come out right, now did it?"

He laughed as he helped her to a bench under a tree. "Not quite what you meant to say, but I understand. Stay here. An hour at the most, I think."

He finally walked towards her, fatigue weighing his feet. He needed to talk to her but he wasn't sure how far he could go.

"Seth, can we go somewhere we can talk?" Her words echoed his. "I'm sorry. I shouldn't have asked that. You need to clean up and have your supper."

"How be I clean up, take you out for a meal, and then we talk? We still have that box to open, don't we?"

"We do." She sighed as she walked with him to his truck. "They were digging again in the town forest. Your mother said they found something there."

"They did. Frank's dog alerted to something and they've been working to excavate the area. I haven't talked to anyone yet to know what they found."

Their meal over, they wandered near the river before Seth pulled her down on a bench that was sheltered.

"You wanted to talk, Faith?"

She nodded. "I did and now I've lost my courage to ask you what I need to ask."

He laughed, a gentle laugh. "Then, may I? I have come to love you, Faith, more than I ever though possible. I don't want to see you walk away from me, to leave me ever."

She had turned her eyes to him as he spook, seeing his feelings on his face. She hesitated, knowing that when she spoke, it would change their world.

"Thank you, Seth. I appreciate those words." She stopped speaking, swallowing hard.

Seth's heart sank. This was it, he thought. She's telling me she's leaving and will never come back. Lord, how do I handle that?

"Seth, you have become so important to me. I hate the thought you could be hurt because of me. But I too love you deeply. That's hard for me to say. I have built a wall to protect myself and you just climbed right over it and took my heart."

He sighed, then bent to kiss her. Cradling her against him finally, he sat, knowing that God had indeed answered his prayer. Here sat, in his arms, the lady he had prayed for all his life, since his father and mother suggested that he pray for his life mate.

"Now what, Seth? We're still not finished Grandmother's hunt? Will it end too?"

"I think it will." He pulled out the box and studied it. "I think it's time we opened this one." He worked at the lid, raising it.

"What's in it this tie?"

"A dried flower." He touched it gently. "And for once I have no idea what it is."

"A landscape artist not knowing his flowers." She peeked at it, a gasp coming from her. "Oh, Grandmother, what have you done?"

"What is it, Faith? Do you recognize it?"

She nodded, through the tears that clouded her eyes. "I do. It's a dried orange blossom. Mom has some from her own headdress when she and Dad married. What was Grandmother thinking?"

"I think she decided you and I belonged together and she wanted to bring us to this point. I can't say for sure that's what her plan was."

Faith started to laugh. "I can see her doing just that. What next?"

"I think one more box. Now, where would this send us?"

"That we'll figure out. Right now, we have other things to talk about."

"Your mother stopped by this morning. She was reading me right, you know."

"I'm sure she was. She has this perception thing going. I can't figure it out, but she knows things without being told."

Faith moved finally. "It's getting dark, Seth. I need to get home to Sara."

He stood, his hand reaching for hers, and then he stopped, his finger tracing her hand. "I need to find you a ring, my love. Something special, just for you."

"Later, Seth. Right now, we need to figure out what she meant by the flower and where we go next."

He laughed. "I'm sure we will."

Chapter 19

Sipping at her coffee the next morning, her eyes on her computer monitor, Faith worked away, part of her mind still trying to determine what her Grandmother had meant by the flower. She sighed, bringing her attention back to the manuscript, finishing off what she needed to do and sending it back to the publisher. She had another waiting for her, but she wanted a break. Her eyes were sore and Sara was demanding she come outside.

Sara raced around, her body having grown in the last few days, Faith thought. She walked through her garden, hands reaching to touch plants growing tall and strong. She paused, her eyes seeking the distance, still feeling like she was being watched.

Calling Sara, she started back for the house, her footsteps slowing before she broke into a run. Sara raced beside her, barking wildly, thinking her mistress had come up with a new game for them to play.

Faith kicked off her shoes and ran for the stairs, almost tripping over Sara as she did so. She slid to a halt at her Grandmother's bedroom door, breathing hard, her heart hammering.

"I think I know where the last box is, Seth. It's here, in her room. I know I saw something one day when I was in here, just looking around, trying to decide what I needed to keep and give away."

She searched the most obvious places, until she reached the carved walnut chest at the foot of the bed. She knelt, her hands running over the carving, remembering now how she had loved it as a child, being fascinated with the flowers and leaves. She leaned closer. Yes, it was as she thought. Orange blossoms and roses were the flowers

"Grandmother, what were you thinking? You were trying to find me someone special, weren't you? You've prayed for this for all my life, I know now. Just like Mom and Dad have." Tears blinded her and she laid her head on the edge of the chest and sobbed. Sara whined, trying to lick at her face, and then just cuddling close, her chin and a front paw on Faith's leg.

How much later, Faith never knew, that she raised her head, wiping away the tears.

She reached for the clasp, gently raising the lid and staring into the chest. She moved aside tissue paper, seeing an old-fashioned wedding veil and then underneath what had once been a beautiful white dress, the silk now ivory with age. Grandmother, you would have been beautiful in this. She felt around the edges, her fingers touching a box that now felt so familiar.

"This is the last one, isn't it, Grandmother? The last one you planned in our hunt. You must have had such fun coming up with this. I wish I had known you as my Grandmother. I have missed out on that. But you knew my heart. You knew I loved you so much."

She fingered the box, seeing a picture of a dog that looked so much like Sara. "This is it, Sara. Whatever is in here is the last clue. Then I'll read her letter. She knew me so well, knew I would never read the letter, not until I had to."

She finally rose, heading for the stairs, seeing Seth's truck just pulling in. Was it that late, she asked herself? Running down the stairs, she stared at the clock. She had been up in her Grandmother's room for hours.

She frantically searched for a meal she could put together quickly, running for the door as she heard Seth calling her.

He searched her face, knowing something had happened, but not questioning her, knowing his lady love would talk when she was ready.

He finally caught her hand and led her to their favourite spot, the prayer bench her Grandmother had used for so long.

"Faith, I did some shopping today. On my lunch hour." He groaned as she laughed at him. "How cliche is that? I found a ring. If you don't like it, I can take it back. I just wanted something special for you, my love." He reached for his pocket, pulling out a ring.

She gasped, her mouth open, before she snapped it close. "Seth? What did you do?"

"I found a ruby for my lady love whose worth is far above rubies." She knew he was quoting from Proverbs 31. They had discussed that the night before. "That's what you are to me. Will you wear it?"

She nodded, her hand going out, watching as he slipped the ring to her finger. "How did you get the right size?"

"I have no idea. It must be one of those God things Mom and Dad talk about." He laughed as she hugged him before he kissed her thoroughly.

Her head on his shoulder, she sighed. "I think this is where I'll spend a lot of time. It has so many memories for us."

He nodded. "You and me both, if you don't mind sharing. I'm guessing we'll be keeping this place and living here."

"If you don't mind. I feel so close to God here. I know Grandmother was a prayer warrior and that she has bathed this place in prayer just for us."

"I think she did." He sat, content for the moment. "How was your day?"

"Good. Quiet. I finished off the one manuscript and returned it. And I found the last box."

She waited for him to comment, a giggle suppressed within her as her words passed over him.

He suddenly stopped, his words dying on his lips as he caught her words. "You found the last box? How? Where?"

"In Grandmother's room. She has a chest that has orange blossoms and roses carved on it. It holds her wedding veil and gown. The box was tucked down inside it."

She paused in her words, a brief sadness washing over her. "This is it, Seth. This is the last one. Once we've opened it, the hunt is over. I'll need to read her letter." She felt for her pocket. "I've been carrying it with me for the last couple of days, knowing we were coming to the end of the hunt."

"I think your Grandmother plotted this. She often asked me if I had a lady, and I would just laugh at her and say no. She must have wanted us to meet, that's why she set this up."

"I think she did. But she was willing to let God have His way." She reached into her pocket, pulling out the box. "Here, you open it. I just can't."

He nodded, his hand on her hair for a moment, before he took the box and worked at the lid. He paused. "This looks like Sara."

"That's what I thought. I wonder if that's why she went with Sara."

"Your Grandmother? You think she's the one?"

"I do. I think she wanted me to have a dog. I have been afraid of dogs for so many years and couldn't say why. Sara changed that for me."

He nodded, his attention back on the box. "Here, let's see what's she given us this time."

He stared down at the box and then at Faith. "Faith, did you know this?"

"Know what?" She leaned over to look. "Oh, my. Grandmother, what did you go and do?" She reached in and pulled out a tiny thin gold band. "This was her ring, Seth. I remember seeing it. She left it for me."

"That she did, love. I think she prayed and hoped that you would find true love. She had certainly hinted at that all along."

Faith nodded. "But I still feel as if there's more to it than this. That there's a treasure she often spoke about that we haven't found in the hunt yet." She looked up. "It's getting dusky, Seth. Let's head for the house."

She stood, having brought out all the boxes and arranged them in the order that they had found them, then looked down at the letter. Seth sat and watched her, compassion on his face.

"It won't bite, my love. Do you want me to read it for you?"

She nodded. "I think so. I don't think I could see to read." She handed it to him.

Not satisfied with that, Seth rose and approached her, pulling out a chair and then cradling her close to him on his knee, knowing that she needed that contact.

"Let's read this and see what she has to say." He prayed first, then opened the envelope and pulled out the folded papers within.

Unfolding them, he watched Faith closely, knowing just how fragile she was at the moment.

"My dearest Faith"

"How I love you, my child. I have been so blessed to have known you, even though we have had to meet like we did. You are such a delight, a real delight to be around. Your Mom has kept me up to date on all that has gone on in your life. I grieve that I could not be the part of it I wanted to be, but perhaps, God had a different plan for us. I know we would not have been this close if it had been different.

"Whatever happened all those years ago, you have never said, have not been able to tell us. We have tried to find out but you just shut down. I pray that at some point you will remember and be able to understand what happened.

"Now, my love, I have prayed for a life mate for you since you were born. I have no idea who that will be but God does. He has the one waiting for you that He alone has chosen.

"If you are reading this, then I have gone on to Heaven, graduated as they say. I will miss you, my darling girl. But if this is the case and you are indeed reading this, then I have confidence that you working through the hunt I sent you on and have found all ten objects.

"You may think that there is only earthly meaning to each one. But I can tell you, as I planned it, God spoke to me. He has laid out each object and its heavenly meaning for you."

Seth paused at that point, hugging Faith tight as she wept. Wept for the past. Wept for her Grandmother. Wept for time lost with her. His own tears wet her hair.

$\mathscr{F}$aith finally settled herself down enough that she could ask Seth to continue to read. At some point, she had reached for Sara and now had her dog cuddled into her arms.

Seth's eyes searched her face and then returned to the letter.

"My darling girl, this is what God has said to me about this hunt.

"Clue 1 - The treasure. God is our treasure. We need to seek Him with all our hearts and minds. He will be found.

"Clue 2 - God does not promise us riches here on earth. He has those stored in heaven for us. He delights to provide for us here though. Sometimes treasures are not physical things. They can be the love of a good man and a family that loves you deeply.

"Clue 3 - You as a child Faith were such a delight. Just remember, that is how we are to approach God - as little children, without any preconceived ideas about what He is like. He delights in our childlike faith, providing glimpses of what heaven will be like.

"Clue 4 - A thimble. What has that to do with our faith? Remember the woman who was ill? She touched the hem of the Master's garment. A garment that was sewn at some. He will bring healing of any kind to us. I pray for that healing for you.

"Clue 5 - A needle. A reminder that riches do not get us into heaven. Only faith in God does - think of the needle gate Christ talked about.

"Clue 6 - The wishing stone. We often wish our lives away, wanting things to be different, running ahead of God and getting ourselves in trouble. When you look at it, remember not to wish for things God does not have in His plans for you.

"Clue 7 - The nail. A reminder of what held Christ to the cross - the nails that drove through His flesh to bring our salvation and healing.

"Clue 8 - Your cross. Again, a reminder of what Christ has accomplished. And that we are to be His witnesses.

"Clue 9 - The orange blossom. A reminder that Christ prayed for us in the

Garden. I know this is a favourite passage of yours.

"Clue 10 - My ring. I no longer have need for it, my darling Faith. But you have found your treasure, if God has willed. You have found a man who sees your worth, treats you as his lady love, and will walk beside you every step of the way home, no matter what you face.

"Faith, my darling. I have come to the end of my walk here on earth. No one knows the days that God had decreed for each one of us. I pray a long, blessed life for you, my darling, with a man who loves you more than life itself. If you have found that, then you have found richness indeed. If God chooses that you walk on your own, put your hand in His, knowing He has you in His hands. Trust Him my love.

"And if Seth Logan has become the man you do love, you have my blessings, many times over. He is a good man, was a good boy, deeply in love with our Lord and Saviour.

"I must close now, my darling girl. Know that I love you deeply.

"Grandmother."

Seth silently folded the letter back into the envelope, carefully setting it on the table, then wrapping his arms tight around his lady, holding her as she sobbed, Sara trying her best to lick away all the tears and make her feel better.

Faith's tears finally subsided. "That is quite the hunt she sent us on. A treasure hunt, in more ways than one."

"That is was, my love. I think she knew we'd meet and fall in love. She had those visions. Mom couldn't never explain it to me, just that someone saw things the rest of us didn't."

"I do that, Seth. I see things that come true. I've always hated that." She leaned back to look up at him. "But now, seeing how Grandmother used it, I think it can be a blessing, not the curse I always felt it."

"That it can be." Seth sat for a while longer before he set her on her feet, rose and caching her under an arm, walked to the door. "Lock up after me. Tomorrow's Saturday. I'll be over early. Let's spend the day together, doing something fun."

"I would like that. Thank you, Seth, for all you've done and who you are."

He smiled before kissing her good night and then walking to his truck. He waited until he saw her lock up and turn off lights before he drove away, his thoughts on the letter and the hunt Grandmother Gordon as he now thought of her as had sent them on. God, is this what it was all about? Somehow, I don't think we're done yet.

Chapter 22

*F*aith watched as Seth ran through the grass with Sara nipping at his heels. She laughed, knowing how much the two loved one another. She had talked to Frank that morning, who confirmed it was her Grandmother who had purchased Sara for her, knowing that she would help to heal Faith's heart.

Faith waved as Seth looked up, pointing to her watch. They had planned to go somewhere for lunch, just to celebrate everything, and she was definitely getting hungry.

Seth swept her into his arms and kissed her, then picked Sara up to carry her to the house, locking her up, making sure she had plenty of water.

"Now, my love. Where to?" He caught her hand as they walked to his truck.

"I have no idea, Seth. Where do you suggest?"

He shrugged, a smile on his face. "There's a stop I'd like to make first, if you're up for it." He held up a finger as she went to speak. "No questions. You'll understand when we get there."

She watched with amusement as he pulled into the church parking lot. "The church? Really? Aren't we a day early for services?"

He laughed heartily at that. "We are, but the pastor's here. I thought we might talk to him for a moment, to see what kind of dates we can come up."

Her steps slowed and then stopped, pulling him back to her. "Seth? A date? As in a wedding date?"

He nodded. "It doesn't have to be soon, but I would like to have some idea of when you'll say I Do."

She shook her head, knowing her life would be one of constant surprises with this man.

"Then, let's go talk to him. You'll also need to talk to Dad." She looked up, seeing his smirk. "You didn't! You did, didn't you? You've already talked to him."

"Let's put it this way. He talked to me a couple of nights before they went home. He wanted to make sure I wouldn't hurt you."

"And that you will never do. I know that, Seth Logan."

A hour later, a list of dates in hand, Seth seated her at a table in a quaint little restaurant in Oak Landing.

"This is nice. It's so cozy, yet private." She looked around with interest.

"It is. We don't come here much, only with special occasion. And I would saw, Miss Webster soon to be Mrs. Logan, that this is definitely a special occasion."

"You're flying high today, aren't you?" She laughed as his enthusiastic nod.

"That I am. Now, what will you have to eat?"

They walked through the downtown area when they were done, browsing through some of the shops, not seeing the men following them. They didn't sense the danger that awaited them. Faith wondered afterwards if they had, would they have avoided what occurred? Seth assured her that none of them could know that.

Later that evening, just as dusk was falling, they headed home, Faith's heart thankful for the day. She knew there was still events she needed to remember and work through.

Seth's concentration was not as sharp as it should been, not watching the vehicles around him. He pulled onto the side road, leading to house, not seeing the truck with its lights suddenly turned off follow him. He didn't see anything until his truck was struck violently from behind, sending it careening off the road and into a ditch. He heard Faith's scream before the doors were wrenched and they were yanked from the vehicle.

Seth staggered, his eyes blurring for a moment, before he straightened, searching for Faith, seeing her being shoved ahead of a man towards the woods. Lord, please save us. He felt the shove and followed his lady, not knowing what they would be walking into and afraid for her. Himself, he didn't care about.

They were finally shoved into a shack, and then down to the floor. Seth reached for Faith, drawing her close to him, his eyes on the men as they stood apart from them, arguing he thought. Now what, Lord?

Faith's breathing finally slowed, her hand grasping Seth's not as tight. She still shook intermittently, fear driving her. She had no idea what these men wanted, and she really just wanted to go home, to find Sara, to cuddle up with her dog and relax. And yes, talk to her Mom and plan her wedding. Now, even that was in doubt. She hated that thought. She wanted to be free and thought she was. Obviously she was wrong, wasn't she, Lord? Then she sighed. No, trust God. That's what Grandmother would say.

She didn't look up as she saw the men's shoes come into her line of sight. She jumped as a hand hit her face, her own hand coming up to the spot, hearing the growl come from Seth before it abruptly cut off.

"Where is it?" The gruff voice was one she recognized. He had been in the barn that day, the day they had hidden behind the straw bales.

A hand clamped onto her shoulder and shook her. "Where is it? I know she left something. Where is it?"

Faith shook her head. "I have no idea what you're looking for. There were just some things that made sense to me, no one else." Her head hit Seth's shoulder as an even more vicious blow hit her face. Her hand clutched his, stopping him from rising, even as she heard his angry words to leave her alone.

"There is. I heard her say something about a treasure. I was outside her house that day for something and I heard her talking. She hid a treasure. I want that."

Faith shook her head, the pain making her blink away tears. "There is no treasure. Not what you think any way?"

"What are you talking about?" The second man spoke, drawing Seth's attention.

"The treasure is in heaven. I'm sorry. There isn't any treasure on earth." Faith's words were low and pity laced them. She turned her face into Seth's shoulder, waiting for what she wasn't sure.

The two men moved away, walking outside. The two left inside could hear them arguing, the argument heated and laden with foul language.

"Seth? What are we to do?" Faith kept her voice low and her face turned to him.

"I don't know, my love. We'll think of something, I'm sure. Now, we just need to keep them from hitting you again."

"It's just a bruise, Seth. It will heal."

"I know, but they shouldn't be hitting you. I'm trying to think of how to get out of here. I know this cabin. It's on Frank's property. We used to play here as young kids." He froze, not liking the way his thoughts were going.

"Frank's not involved, Seth. I know he's not."

"I hope not. But his cousin is. That's the second man, Fred. He's always been just this side of being on the wrong side of the law."

"Now, it looks as if he's crossed that line." She peeked at the door and then around the cabin. "It's too dark to see if we can get out."

"We can't. Not yet. Here, slide down and put your head on my leg. Maybe if they think you're really hurt, they won't touch you again."

"We can try that, but somehow I don't think it will work all that well." She did as he asked, her hand reaching for his. "Seth, God will get us out of this. That I know."

"Yes, I know He will." But how, he wondered? Would it be dead or alive? With what he'd been hearing lately about Fred and knowing Frank's concern for his cousin, Seth worried it would be the later. He leaned back against the wall, his arm around his lady, his eyes sliding closed. He didn't see or hear the two men return, didn't hear the curses of the first one before he turned and stormed from the cabin, leaving Fred to stand and stare at the young couple, before he shook his head and walked out, finding a seat on the porch, pulling his hat down over his eyes, and dozing off.

The other man headed for their truck, and then stopping to look at Seth. He climbed into Seth's, hiding it in the trees, before he returned to his own. He needed something that wasn't in the cabin. He needed his bottle and that was in his hotel room.

Chapter 23

Faith roused the next morning, finding her head on Seth's jacket and not seeing Seth anywhere around her. She sprang to her feet, her eyes searching for him, a hand to her throat. Where are you?

She heard a sound and turned, searching for it, seeing boards moving at the window at the back of the cabin. Seth, she could now hear, was out front, an argument going on around him, his voice speaking in a calm, reasoned manner. She crept to the front window, seeing him standing there, hands thrust into his jeans pockets, not moving from where he was standing. She could tell he was thinking, looking for a way out and not finding one.

She turned at a sudden creak behind her. Frank was at the window, beckoning her to come. She crept towards him.

"Frank? What are you doing here?" Her voice was low.

"Out you come, Faith. I got word you were here. We're working on getting Seth out as well. For now, we need you to come with us." He reached through the window, lifting her up and out and then grabbing her hand to run for the trees, his head turned slightly to watch behind him.

"Frank. Stop!" Faith finally pulled her hand free and halted. "What is going on? Why are you here? Isn't that your cousin who is one of our abductors?"

Frank blew out a breath. "It is, Faith. He's not a bad guy, if that's what you're thinking. I can't explain, but he got word to me last night to come and get you. He'll help Seth get away. His main concern was you." Frank grabbed her hand again and pulled her with him. "We need to put space between us and them. Don't worry. The police are moving in now, even as we're heading away. I was to get you out and then they'd move in. That was the request Fred made."

He grabbed her hand once more and pulled her along with him. Her breath coming in pants, her legs screaming with pain from the exertion, she finally pulled her hand free and dropped to the ground, her face buried in her hands. "I can't go on, Frank. I need to rest." Her eyes turned back to where the cabin was. "Why here, Frank? Why me?"

"That's what we're figuring out. The older man. Fred says he overhead something about a treasure your Grandmother was hiding. He's greedy, looking for a score that will let him live high and mighty without having to worry about money. He doesn't know your Grandmother never had the riches on earth he thinks she did."

"We all know that. How could he not?"

"That's what we'll find out." He reached for her hand. "I've taken you on a circuitous route to my place. You'll be safe there, for now. Fred says there were only the two of them. He's been able to keep the other guy in line for now, but something triggered this attack on you two last night."

"And I think I know why. He would have heard that we found the last box and had found the treasure." She sighed, then swiped at the tears on her face. "Please, Frank. Make sure Seth makes it back to me. I can't lose anyone else I love."

Frank gave a quick grin as he pushed her down at his kitchen table and then reached to make them a hot drink, sticking bread into a toaster. "It's like that, is it?"

She held up her hand, her ring sparkling on her finger. "He gave me this. We had talked to the pastor yesterday about dates.

We've settled on one but this changes it. I don't want to lose him. Please, Frank!"

He watched for a moment, before reaching into a drawer, pulling out a small hand towel that he dampened and handed to her. He moved to let his Shelties loose. Sara's mother, Daisy, watched Faith for a moment before she padded over and stood up at her leg, her nose finding Faith's face, and her tongue coming out to lick at her cheek.

Faith gave a choked cry and then reaching down, swept the dog into her arms, her thick coat soaking up her fresh tears.

Frank let her weep, knowing she needed it, but also knowing he would soon need to talk to her. They had to make plans, just in the event Seth didn't make it out right away and Fred headed his way to warn him. He had to be ready to get her out of there. And he would. That he had promised her Grandmother. That he would watch out for her and protect her. He had tried to do just that. With her memory coming back, he knew it was a matter of time before she recalled what had happened all those years ago. He too had heard the rumours and knew that if she remembered and the wrong people caught wind of that, she would never survive. That much he knew.

He finally drew her up and to the couch in the kitchen, making her lay down, drawing the blanket over her, watching as Sara's mother jumped up and curled up behind her knees, her chin on Faith's legs, watchful, knowing something was wrong with this lady, the one she could smell Sara on.

Frank paced, the time passing slowly. Where are you, Seth? It can't be taking this long to get you free. It's been two hours now since I walked off with Faith. Fred, please don't let him die. Faith will never survive if he does.

He turned finally, hearing the door knob turn. Fred stood there, dishevelled, bloody and with a look on his face that stopped Frank in his tracks.

"Fred?"

Fred nodded at Sara. "Can you wake her? We need to get her to the hospital. Seth was hurt. He's been asking for her."

Frank waited. "And?" He finally asked.

"It's over, Frank. Finally, it's over. I can come home and be the person I've always been, not the person everyone thought I was."

"And for that I am so glad." Thank you, Father, he breathed as he turned, his hand on Faith's shoulder, shaking her away, seeing the fear in her eyes as her gaze found Fred.

"He's alive, Faith. Fred just came to get us. Come on, lady. On your feet. Let's get you to him." He spoke to the dog. "Sorry, Daisy. You can't come. I know you've staked your claim on Faith, but she has to leave. Don't worry. I'm sure she'll come back to visit. If not, I know where she lives and I'll take you to her."

Faith ran for the hospital entrance, her heart in her mouth, seeking to find where Seth was. The clerk was not at her desk, and Faith spun in a circle, trying to find someone who could tell her how Seth was. She stopped as she felt an arm come around her. Joseph had stopped her movements and drew her to where Martha stood waiting, her arms out to welcome Faith.

"Have you heard anything?" Faith's words tumbled over one another.

"Not yet. The paramedics said he wasn't hurt too badly but that he needed to be assessed. They'll come get us when they can." Her hands caught Faith's, stilling the younger woman's movements. "They know, Faith. They know you're the most important person to him. You'll go in first."

"No, you both need to come with me. I can't go in on my own." Fear tightened her face. "It's too much like when I got the call about Mom's accident. Dad was away overnight and it was just me. Just me waiting, all by myself. I didn't think to call anyone to come."

Joseph and Martha shared a horrified look, finally realizing just how much this would traumatize her.

"Oh, Faith. We never thought. We didn't know where you were. We were just told you were safe. If we had known, we would have come for you." Joseph reached for his handkerchief, handing it to Faith, watching as she swiped at her cheeks, then sat, eyes on the door to the rooms, twisting the handkerchief in her hands.

Martha hugged her to her, knowing that Eva would be there if she could. Joseph had spoke to Paul, learning that Eva had had to come back in the hospital for some more testing, but that they would be there as soon as they could. He hoped to be on the road to his daughter that very afternoon. He knew Eva would leave the hospital without her testing done if he told her.

Faith was on her feet and across the room as she saw the physician heading for them.

"Doctor. Seth?"

"You're his lady? Faith? He's asking for you. He's fine. Shaken up. Bruised and battered but in one piece. He got a cut on his arm we had to stitch up but other than that he's free to go once the IV is finished. Here, the nurse will take you back."

Faith almost ran to find Seth, leaving Joseph and Martha to hurry after her. They found her in Seth's arm, sobs wracking her body, tears on his face. He reached up a hand for his parents and then hugged his lady tighter and tighter.

Faith finally stood back. "I was so afraid. Frank took me out the window and to his place."

"I know. That's what Fred wanted him to do." Seth nodded at his father. "Fred has never been the person he was portrayed to be. He's been working to solve a few mysteries here around town."

Joseph nodded. "That's what your Mom and I have always figured. He has had too good a heart to be bad." He looked at Faith, seeing the fatigue in her face. "Now, when are you ready to leave? You're both coming back to our place. I stopped by this morning and used the key your Grandmother had given me years ago, Faith. Sara's at our place."

"Thank you." She watched as the nurse removed the IV needled and helped Seth to sit up, helping him to the wheelchair and then into Joseph's car, tight to him and with her hand in his as they headed for home.

Chapter 24

*F*aith's screams had everyone out of bed in the middle of the night. Seth pounded on her door and then, with no response, shoved it open and searched for her, finding her sitting in the middle of the bed, her arms over her head in a protective manner, the screams shaking her body.

He approached, sitting carefully beside her, his voice as calm as he could make it, fear and worry shaking him to his core. Martha sat on her other side, a hand touching her back, soothing words flowing from her. When it was all over, Martha could not have told them what words she had spoken, only that God had spoken through her.

Faith gradually calmed, her eyes first on Martha, then sensing Seth beside her, she turned and was in his arms, her own arms tight enough around his neck he had trouble breathing. He whispered words meant only for her, words that she would recall later that had calmed her and reassured her. She sat back, her terror lessening, a sense of having done this before coming over her, shame at having awakened everyone else showing on her face.

Joseph had stood, leaning against the wall, just watching. He sighed, wishing it was Paul that was here right then, but knowing he would have to play the father role, to comfort and reassure her.

He crouched downing front of her, his hands held palm up, until she reached for them and he gripped hers.

"It's okay, Faith. I think you've finally broken through that last barrier. Last night was the final part you needed to understand what happened. Is that correct?"

She nodded, her eyes sad. "It was, Joseph. It was. I finally see what I saw all those years ago. It terrifies me. I need to go home."

Seth held her in place. "Not now, Faith. It's still the middle of the night. I'll take you home as soon as it's light. Then, we can talk through what happened. You do remember everything?"

She nodded. "I do." She shoved at him. "I'm not going to sleep. Let me up."

He moved, watching as she moved away, heading for the main floor. His mother stopped his forward movement with a hand on his arm.

"Let her go, Seth. She needs this time. Let your Dad go. She needs her father right now and he's not here. He won't be here until tomorrow, as much as he wanted to be here."

Seth finally nodded, walking to the top of the stairs and finding a place where he could sit, his feet on a stair below him, his shoulder again the railing, as he listened to his lady move restlessly around the house, his heart broken for her but raised in prayer.

His father touched his shoulder as he moved past him, his thoughts intent on the lady his son loved. His heart breaking for both of them, he prayed as he had not prayed in years.

Faith finally moved to the kitchen, reaching for the tea Joseph handed her.

Her voice hoarse, she could barely speak her thanks.

"That's okay, Faith. We all knew this was coming. I think you'll find your Grandmother made plans for just this."

"I think she did. How she would and what that would be, I have no idea." She sat at the table, her hands twisting her mug in a restless motion. "But what she planned. I have no idea." She finally looked up at him, ready to apologize.

"No. No apologies. Family doesn't apologize for something like this. And you're just about as close to family as you can."

She smiled her thanks, her thoughts returning over the past few weeks. "Joseph, do you know what happened the statue in the garden?"

"The girl and dog one? Now, that's a puzzle. It was there the day I found your Grandmother but when I had to go back later that day, it had been moved. I have no idea who or why."

She shrugged at that. "I was just wondering. We can't find it and we think it's the final piece of the puzzle."

"That it may well be. Listen. It's light now. Let Seth talk you home and you get showered and changed and then come back here. Your parents will be in this afternoon at some point."

"Thank you for calling them. I never thought to do that, not until Dad called." She shuddered. "I was so glad to hear his voice."

Seth watched later as Faith moved around her house, picking up objects and then replacing them. He finally stood in her way and when she looked up at him, simply wrapped her into his arms, his cheek on her hair.

"It's okay, love. You have to grieve, more than one thing. When you're ready, we'll talk."

"I think I'm at that point now, Seth. Can we go outside? I'm so restless I can't stay still. Maybe if we walked or spent time around the garden, I'll get myself back to where I need to be."

"Sure. Let's go." They headed for the back of the house, stopping at her garden.

She stared at it, sensing something different.   Then, her hand gripped Seth's tighter. "Seth. In the centre."

He had been watching her face and when she paled, he looked towards where she was pointing, then walked that way, Faith keeping step with him.

"It's back. The statue. Now, how did that happen?" Seth was puzzled.

Faith knelt, her hands on the statue of the girl and dog, one of the girl's hands on the dog, the other holding a closed book on her knee. "Whoever it was that was working with Grandmother did this. I don't know who and I'm not sure I want to know. But God has returned it to me, Seth." She looked up, this time with no tears, but a smile of happiness.

"It looks like you and Sara." Seth crouched down, his hands touching the statue, before he frowned. He leaned forward, finding a letter attached to it. "Faith, here's another letter."

"Not another one! Oh, I pray it's not bad news."

Seth smiled at that, then handed her the letter. She shook her head. "You open it. I can't."

He did just that, finding only a card inside. He opened that, surprise colouring his face.

"Faith, I think you need to read this yourself. It's a message just for you."

"It can't be that personal." She watched as Seth nodded, before taking the card. "Let's see, then." She read, her face paling as she finished before she looked up at him. "Grandmother did that? How could she have done that?"

"I don't know, love, but now we know what she was really up to. She wanted you to find the real treasure first and then this." He reached to pull her up to her feet, and with an arm around her, turned her towards the creek. "I think we need to find your Grandmother's prayer corner."

"I think we do." Faith said, her eyes back on the card. "I never knew this, you know. I didn't know she was wealthy, not like this. Mom never said."

"I think you'll find your mother never knew. This is likely from investments she made in the last few years. From what I understand she had talked to Dad and a few other men in the church, asking their counsel."

"I don't know what to do with this. I'll leave it where it is for now."

"Not so fast, girlie. That money's mine. You'll hand it all over."

Faith screamed as the voice sounded behind her, flying to her feet and away from the bench, spinning to see who it was.

"I thought you were in custody. How'd you get away?"

"It takes more than that to keep me in jail. Now, hand over the money." The older male captor stood there, a weapon pointed at Faith as he held out a hand.

"I can't. I don't have it yet. And I won't get it, not to hand it over to you."

"Then, we'll wait until tomorrow when the bank opens, we'll go into together and you'll hand it all over to me."

Faith shook her head. "I don't think so. That's not happening." She had heard the sounds of footsteps heading their way and glanced at Seth. She couldn't tell if he had heard them or not.

Seth waited, his eyes on the man, watching until the weapon was turned from Faith before he had a move.

"Faith, run!" Seth launched himself at the man, his hand clamped around the man's wrist as he fought for control of the weapon. A lucky blow with his other hand sent the weapon spiralling through the air to land with a splash in the creek.

A cry of outrage sounded from the man and he drew back a heavy fist, the crunch of it on Seth's jaw sounding through the air. Seth dropped to the ground, groans pulled from deep within him. The man searched for the weapon, rising to stand still, his hands rising as he saw the officers surrounding him, their own weapons on him.

Faith flew to Seth's side, her arms raising him from the ground, her eyes on him. She knew he had been hurt, from the pain on his face.

"Seth? Are you all right?"

He shook his head, pain sending his eyes closed as he gave way to it, his body relaxing in Faith's arm. She gave a cry, alerting the officers to his plight.

Hours later, she once more stood at his hospital bedside, watching as he grumbled away, pain and fatigue and a touch of anger on his face.

"You can't leave tonight, Seth. You've just had surgery to wire your jaw shut. So lay back and relax."

He glared at her words, before he sighed and nodded, his hand reaching for her. The blow from the man indeed fractured his jaw and he had had to have surgery to wire it together. He was worried about Faith, even though they had been reassured that everyone was now in custody.

Faith finally walked away for the night, her father and mother flanking her. She was safe at last, the terror from her childhood finally explained and her heart in the hands of the man she loved and who loved her deeply.

She raised her face to the stars, thanking God and then adding a request that He tell her Grandmother all was well, at long last.

A month later, Faith searched for Seth, not seeing him around. Their wedding was in a week and they had decided to go over the last minute plans. Her Grandmother's dress and veil had been brought out of the chest and fitted to her. She was happy, but there was still some questions she felt only Seth could help her answer. She called for Sara and headed for the creek, knowing just where she'd find him.

He raised a hand as he saw her, his jaw still sore although the wires had been removed earlier that week. She slid closer to him as she sat, his arm around her, her head on his shoulder, Sara on their feet. They sat for a while, before Faith spoke.

"I still have some questions and I'm not sure we'll ever have the answers for them."

"I think I know what some of them are." He nodded to the horizon. "The man who abducted us, Earl Unger? That was his brother. From what Earl said, they argued and he shoved him. His brother fell and struck his head. A fatal blow from what the medical examiner can determine. We think you saw it, made a noise and he saw you and threatened you. You shut down, your terror was that great. It has taken all these years and coming back to here for that memory to rise to the surface and let you put it to rest."

"That's what happened. It's all so clear to me now. I did shut down. I had such terror about coming back here and had no idea why. Poor Grandmother. If I had only remembered, we could have had such a different life."

"You've had the life God meant you to have. That's a given. Both you and your Grandmother were in His hands. He could have allowed you to remember at any time but didn't."

She sighed. "I know. I wonder where the statue was all that time."

"In the barn. Dad said he talked to the youth who helped Grandmother and promised he would never tell his name. The youth didn't think anything about your Grandmother setting up a scavenger hunt. It's like we figured. He thought it was for the youth group, but continued with her instructions even after her death. She had been specific about where and when the boxes were placed and the statue returned to the garden."

She laughed. "I can see Grandmother making him do just that, scaring him in the process."

Seth laughed with her. "That I can. Now that we know who was after us, have finished the scavenger hunt, and had the statue returned to the garden, do you think life will be sane for us?"

She shrugged, before she turned to look up at him. "I have no idea what God has planned, but I'm going along for the ride. It can only be interesting." She paused, her eyes searching him. "I am so thankful that she made me return here. I wouldn't have found you. And about the money? I'd like to start some scholarships for local youths with it. I think she'd like that."

"I know she would, my love. And I too am glad you came here. My life would be so empty without you." He kissed her and then turned her face to watch the setting sun, knowing that this was only one of many such evenings they would spend together.

Dear readers

Thank you for choosing the story of Faith and Seth and her garden. It has been different for me to write, not the strong suspense that I love.

Gardens have always been a big part of my life. My mother loved her gardens and passed that love on to me. Her father had a huge garden I remember as a child, with 32 rose bushes. I can still see him wandering around them, his hands clasped behind his back.

A scavenger hunt just seemed a fun thing to start with but it evolved to such a strong part of the plot. Who would have guessed it would? But that happens. Something small can change and become so central to the story.

Shetland Sheepdogs, or Shelties as they are lovingly called, are a huge part of my life. I have three, a sable girl, Emma, a tri-coloured boy named Liam, and tricoloured girl named Natalie. The way Daisy and Sara acted are just the way my three act. Emma loves to curl up behind my legs. They try so hard to make me better. My wonderful Sheltie breeder friend has a blue-merle girl named Sarah. This female was prominent in our thoughts as I was writing as she had a four-puppy litter this week. It was a hat's off to Heather and her Sarah that named Sara in the book.

John 17 - this is a favourite passage of Scripture. I can see Christ on His knees in the garden, knowing what was coming, but loving us so much He prayed for each one of us. How amazing and humbling is that?

Faith and Seth faced dangers but had fun with the scavenger hunt. That is something I'd like to do one day. Their hunt for a treasure turned up two. One a heavenly one as delineated by her Grandmother's clue. The other one was their love for each other, a treasure neither expected to find.

God's blessings on you all.

Ronna

www.ingramcontent.com/pod-product-compliance
Lightning Source LLC
Chambersburg PA
CBHW070457200726
48293CB00007B/2263